SHOCK AND AWE

LANTERN BEACH GUARDIANS, BOOK 2

CHRISTY BARRITT

LANTERN BEACH POLICE Chief Cassidy Chambers had seen a lot of crime scenes, but she'd never witnessed one with this much blood.

She glanced around the small rental house named *Seacret Escape* and frowned.

This one-story cottage was definitely holding on to some secrets that the owner had probably never foreseen when naming the place.

The gruesome scene wasn't what Cassidy had been expecting when she arrived. Not here. Not on her peaceful little island. And the scent . . . the sweet metallic odor made her stomach turn.

Officer Jonathan Banks, one of the newer recruits on the force, turned away as if he couldn't stomach the sight—or smell—of the room surrounding them.

He'd been the one who responded to the call, and he'd been waiting for her to arrive.

"What happened here, Chief?" His voice sounded thinner, more fragile than usual. Though her officer was strong and fit, Banks was also still young and had a lot to learn. His baby face only made him seem more innocent than he probably desired.

"What happened here is exactly what we need to figure out." Cassidy clenched her jaw until a sharp pain shot down her neck. She tried to loosen her muscles, but a kink remained between her ear and neck.

Someone had lost *a lot* of blood. If this person had *somehow* survived his or her injuries, he or she couldn't have gotten very far from this place.

"There's no dead body?" Cassidy clarified.

She didn't want to have tunnel vision and focus on only one theory while excluding all other possibilities. But her gut told her that someone had died here.

"I checked the rest of the house before I called you," Banks said. "No one is here. I was careful not to disturb anything, just like you told me."

Cassidy frowned at the confirmation that their victim was nowhere to be seen.

Two housecleaners waited outside in their car. They'd discovered the scene when they came this morning to clean after the guest staying here had called to say she was checking out.

Cassidy released a long breath, knowing just how overwhelming the task ahead of her would be.

The inside of the place was open concept with the living room, kitchen, and dining area all flowing into each other. From Cassidy's vantage point near the door, she could see that two sea-glass green lamps had been broken. A distressed white coffee table was split down the middle. White linen curtains had been pulled off the wall.

Even stranger . . . based on the way that the blood had darkened and dried, Cassidy guessed that at least twenty-four hours had passed since the crime happened.

But if that was the case, did it mean the perp responsible for this had called the rental office? But if someone had done so . . . that person had to know that cleaners would come to the cottage to prepare it for the next guests to arrive.

Someone had *wanted* them to find this scene—looking just like this.

That fact did nothing to comfort her.

And if the victim had been assaulted here more

than twenty-four hours ago, why had someone waited until today to call the rental agency and say she was checking out?

The questions swirled in her head.

Cassidy turned back to Banks. "We need to document every inch of this house, brush for prints, look for fibers. We can't let anything slip past."

"Understood."

"Can you question the housecleaners while I start to process this?"

"I'd be happy to."

"I hope you didn't have plans for this afternoon or evening."

Banks shrugged. "I did have a date, but . . ."

"I'm sorry, but it doesn't look like that's going to happen. Hopefully she's understanding."

"She can be—sometimes. Either way, duty calls. I'll do whatever's needed."

Banks wasn't the only one who would have to cancel his plans.

Even though it was barely lunchtime now, Cassidy would need to tell her husband, Ty, that she wouldn't be making it home for dinner tonight either.

She'd been looking forward to trying out a new fish taco recipe. Afterward, she and Ty had planned on putting a puzzle together with Annabeth, the six-year-old who was staying with them until her parents could bring her home.

But, as Banks said, duty called.

Cassidy needed to figure out what kind of nightmare had played out here. There was no time to waste.

CASSIDY TOOK one last picture of the scene before using the sleeve of her police uniform to push some stray blonde hairs from her face. Though it was only May, the inside of the cottage was stuffy. And the scent . . . it almost seemed like a physical being bent on slowing her down.

Using police tape, Cassidy had established a perimeter around the outside of the house to contain any relevant evidence. Doc Clemson, the town doctor and medical examiner, had stopped by to confirm how old the blood might be. He'd agreed that it was anywhere between twenty-four and thirty-six hours. He also agreed that someone who'd lost this much blood most likely hadn't survived.

When he'd left, Cassidy had sketched a diagram of the scene before processing the cottage. She'd identified potential evidence with markers, and she'd photographed each piece. She had to be careful to follow a clear chain of custody.

But one thing bothered her—one thing other than the fact that the victim was nowhere to be found.

No personal belongings had been left here.

What sense did that make?

A shadow filled the doorway, and Cassidy looked up to see Officer Braden Dillinger step inside. He and Officer Bradshaw had been assisting at an auto accident earlier and unable to come.

"Paige called and said I was needed here. Bradshaw's wrapping up the fender bender." Dillinger flinched as he glanced around the room. "Wow."

For a former sniper to be nearly speechless only drove home the point that this scene was grisly.

"Wow is right." Cassidy surveyed the space again, feeling like she'd missed something.

Her eyes stopped on the fireplace. She hadn't checked that yet, mostly because people didn't generally use them this time of year. Those who did, more often than not, had gas, and this one was wood burning.

She hurried across the room and leaned down to look into it.

Based on the fresh ashes, someone had used this recently.

"Chief?" Dillinger asked.

"Take a look." She motioned for him to come closer. "But put booties on first."

Her officers hadn't been confronted with many crime scenes like this. Though they knew the protocol, reminders never hurt.

Cassidy pulled a pen from her tool kit and lifted something from the ashes.

"What's that?" Dillinger paused beside her, blue Tyvek covering his black shoes.

"It looks like a leather purse strap to me," Cassidy murmured.

Dillinger squinted. "What . . . ? Why . . . ?"

"My guess is that the person who did this burned the victim's personal belongings."

"That's . . . extreme."

"It seems like someone didn't want us to know the victim's identity," Cassidy said. "And he or she is playing a game with us."

"A game?"

"It's the only reason this person would have called the vacation management company to say the guest had checked out—especially considering when the crime occurred. He wanted us to find this scene before too much time had passed." Cassidy nudged something else. "This looks like a piece of upholstery, maybe from an overnight bag. We're going to need to collect all this."

"I can help." Dillinger knelt beside her. "But where's the body?"

The knot in Cassidy's neck twisted tighter. "That's the question of the day. Doc Clemson and I both believe there's no way someone could have survived losing this much blood."

This wasn't a crime of passion. Based on what Cassidy was seeing, this crime had been carefully planned and executed.

Her blood went cold at the thought.

Two people came to Cassidy's mind when she thought about who might be capable of something like this. Two people who were capable of leaving such a clean crime scene. Two people who'd made sure that Cassidy had found the things they'd wanted her to find. Even the blood left behind had been untouched, except for one area on the living room rug.

This seemed like a crime fit for someone like Lars and Emma Shackleford.

Cassidy had dealt with the couple just over a week ago when they'd posed as Annabeth's parents and tried to retrieve the child from the island. Thankfully, Cassidy had caught on to what they were doing before it was too late. But the two had escaped before she could take them into custody.

When she'd looked into the couple's background, she'd discovered the two had previously worked for the CIA and were now mercenaries for hire.

Could this scene be their doing?

Banks stepped back into the cottage, one hand shoving his phone into his pocket and the other holding a notepad. "I have a name from that rental agreement."

Cassidy stood and turned toward the officer. Her breath caught with anticipation of what he might have discovered. Based on Banks' tone, she was going to want to hear this.

"Go ahead," she said.

His gaze flickered to meet hers. "I'd say you need to sit down for this but . . ."

"I think I can handle it."

"The name of the person renting the house this week was . . . Alexandria Manchester."

Cassidy's head began to spin.

Alexandria Manchester?

Annabeth's mom?

But the woman was missing. Authorities—including Cassidy—had been looking for her for more than a week.

Could Alexandria have been staying on Lantern Beach this whole time, right under their noses?

Even worse . . . was she the one who'd died in this cottage?

CHAPTER TWO

THOUGH CASSIDY COULD HAVE TRUSTED one of her guys to fingerprint the cottage, she wanted to do it herself. That way if anything was missed, she'd have only herself to blame.

A scene like this *should* have plenty of prints.

But the door handle had been wiped clean. The windowsills were clear. The kitchen counter was spotless other than the blood.

Whoever had done this had been careful to cover his or her tracks. Cassidy had even searched the outside of the cottage for blood drips leading away from the house—a sign that the victim had either been carried or somehow walked away.

There was nothing.

She'd searched the shower drains for any signs of blood.

There were none.

That made Cassidy think about the Shacklefords again.

A chill traveled up her spine.

Cassidy had desperately prayed Alexandria Manchester would be found unharmed. She'd prayed that Joe Manchester would awaken from his coma. She prayed that Annabeth would be reunited with them again soon.

But none of those things had happened yet, and the possibilities seemed further away all the time.

Grief clutched her chest. Cassidy couldn't tell Annabeth that her mom was dead. She couldn't. She *wouldn't* until she knew with absolute certainty.

Despite Annabeth's inability to speak, the girl was delightful. Cassidy and Ty had bonded with her quickly—maybe too quickly. Cassidy already knew a hole would remain in her heart when the girl left them one day.

Doc Clemson called Annabeth's condition traumatic mutism. Cassidy didn't know what the girl had been through before she and Ty had found her, but Cassidy could only imagine it was horrible. Annabeth and her parents had been abducted and held on a boat.

With the help of a few friends, Ty and Cassidy made sure that Annabeth was safe here on the island after they'd discovered her washed up on shore, cold and alone. Though the person behind the crimes against Annabeth's family had been apprehended, Cassidy knew others were involved.

Ty's colleagues rotated shifts and stationed themselves outside the house each night to ensure the bad guys didn't return.

She wasn't sure what these people's end game was or what they hoped to get out of the situation.

But something was going on here. Something dark. Something twisted.

Cassidy stepped outside to get some fresh air. It was spring, and the weather was as moody as a woman going through menopause. One moment, the skies were nice and the temperature balmy. The next, the atmosphere turned stormy and the breeze cool. Dark clouds could pop up at any moment—as could the sun.

Right now, it was bright outside, but the breeze felt unseasonably sharp. No doubt, a new weather system was brewing in the distance. They always did around Lantern Beach.

She paced to Banks, who was combing the exterior of Seacret Escape for footprints. But the landscape was mostly sand, and today's wind had likely blown any evidence away. Still, they needed to be certain.

Banks stood from where he'd been crouching near the ground beneath a window. "Nothing yet."

Cassidy frowned, though the news didn't surprise her. "Keep looking. We need to figure out if there was any forced entry into the house."

"Will do. If there's anything out here, I'll find it."

Her gaze went to the driveway where her SUV and two patrol cars were parked, and a new question slammed into her mind.

"Where's the victim's car?" she murmured.

"I was wondering that myself."

Had the killer used it for his getaway? If that was the case, how had the killer gotten here? Had he walked? Had two people worked together on this crime?

That would give more credence to Cassidy's theory about the Shacklefords.

"I need to leave for a moment," Cassidy said. "In the meantime, stay here and guard the scene. Absolutely no one can come or go. Do you understand?"

"Yes, Chief." Banks offered a curt nod.

With that said, Cassidy climbed into her SUV.

Had Alexandria Manchester really been staying here?

That's what Cassidy needed to figure out.

CASSIDY DROVE to the office of Dream Beach Vacation Home Rentals. The owner—a woman named Rebecca Marks, whom Cassidy considered a casual friend—agreed to meet her there.

The building wasn't far from the police station and had been designed to look like an old-school beach cottage with its dormers and cedar siding. An ample parking lot allowed vacationers to pull in and wait until their beach house was sanitized and ready for occupancy.

Rebecca met Cassidy at the front door. The woman, a pretty blonde, was dressed business casual in linen pants and a white top. The office was nearly empty right now, but in three days, when vacation day turnover took place, it would be bustling.

"Florence and Noreen called me." Rebecca frowned as she pushed the door open. "They were so upset."

Cassidy remembered the shock still gripping the

housecleaners when she'd spoken to them after pulling up to the scene. One of them—the crew leader—had trembled all over. The other, a younger woman, looked so pale that Cassidy had almost called an ambulance for her.

"It was a horrible scene." Cassidy stepped into the lobby area where the scent of sea salt and clean cotton surrounded her, offering a brief moment of comfort and normalcy. "I'm sorry they had to experience that."

"I feel so badly for them." Rebecca drew in a heavy breath as she turned to Cassidy in the lobby area. "Now, what do you need from me? Whatever I can do to help you get to the bottom of this. I'm so tired of crimes marring the wholesomeness of this island."

Cassidy snapped into business mode. "When someone rents a cottage from your company, what kind of information do they have to give you?"

"They fill out a form and give us their credit card for any incidentals. We also scan their driver's license. Would you like to see the paperwork of the woman who rented Seacret Escape?"

"That would be great."

Cassidy followed Rebecca into her office and waited as the woman looked through several files.

Finally, she handed one to Cassidy, a wrinkle of worry between her eyes.

"Should I be concerned?" Rebecca pressed her lips together and frowned. "Not just about the mental health of my two housecleaners, but about what's happening on the island?"

Just a week ago, the North Carolina governor had nearly been assassinated here. Tension had remained in the air since then. It was no wonder Rebecca was worried. Who in their right mind wouldn't be?

Cassidy gripped the file and softened her voice. "I don't know yet. That's what we're trying to figure out. But we do believe, at least initially, that these crimes have been very targeted and that everyday citizens and visitors should be safe."

Rebecca's shoulders relaxed some. "Well, that's a relief. I think."

Cassidy opened the folder and looked inside.

Each form had been filled out online, so there were no handwriting samples—nothing to potentially match with Alexandria Manchester's scrawl.

But Cassidy stopped on the photo ID.

Her breath caught.

That was definitely Alexandria's driver's license.

Cassidy had seen it before when she'd researched Annabeth's parents.

The woman had straight, dark hair to her chin. A slim face. Brown eyes. She was thirty-three years old, and she appeared neat and reserved.

But *was* the person who'd checked in here at the agency the real Alexandria? Or had someone stolen her license and credit card and checked in under her name?

Last Cassidy had heard, Alexandria was being held captive. If she was free, certainly she would come find her daughter.

So maybe someone had assumed the woman's identity.

That seemed like a more likely theory.

But right now, that's all it was. A theory.

Cassidy glanced at Rebecca, who stood near her desk studying Cassidy's expression without apology. Cassidy couldn't blame her. The woman had a toddler at home. She was worried about the state of things in her community.

Cassidy raised the folder. "I'm going to need to take a copy of this to the station."

Rebecca nodded. "Of course. Whatever you need."

"Meanwhile, do you have security footage of people coming into the office?"

"We have a camera in our lobby. Would you like me to find the footage from when Mrs. Manchester checked in?"

"If you don't mind, that would be great."

As Rebecca began clicking on her computer, Cassidy's phone buzzed.

She didn't recognize the number, but the area code was from North Carolina.

She put the phone to her ear. "Chief Cassidy Chambers."

Silence stretched.

"Hello?" Cassidy said.

Bad connections weren't unusual on the island.

The next moment, a gravelly voice said, "We know who you are."

The blood drained from Cassidy's face at the ominous words. "Who is this?"

But before she finished the question, a click filled the line.

The caller was gone.

Panic swirled inside her.

Did those words mean what Cassidy thought they did? Did someone really know her true identity? Or was her paranoia simply heightened? Maybe this was something totally unrelated to her past.

Cassidy wasn't sure.

But suddenly, she felt like she was walking on a tightrope over the deep trenches of the ocean and if she fell a turbulent whirlpool would consume her.

CHAPTER THREE

CASSIDY WAITED as Rebecca searched her computer for the security footage from when the supposed Alexandria Manchester checked in.

In the meantime, she tried to get that phone call out of her head.

We know who you are.

Another shiver cascaded down Cassidy's spine as she replayed the words.

Could someone really know her true identity?

If so, the life Cassidy had built here on Lantern Beach would be destroyed.

The air left her lungs as worry seized her.

Cassidy couldn't risk putting Ty and everyone else she cared about in danger, all because of decisions she'd made a lifetime ago. But with so little information, how could she stop anything that might have been put in motion?

"It's right here." Rebecca pointed at the screen.

Cassidy snapped back to the present and looked at the computer. She watched as a dark-haired female came onto the screen.

The grainy image quality wouldn't offer much.

Nonetheless, she wanted to see it.

Rebecca stood and made room for Cassidy. As she did, Cassidy slipped into the seat at the desk and leaned forward.

The video showed a woman amble toward the front desk, glancing around the lobby as she did.

Almost as if she were nervous.

The woman's size and build seem to fit that of Alexandria Manchester. Her hair color was the same, and even the cut matched.

The two women *did* look similar. Eerily similar. But Cassidy couldn't say with certainty that this was Annabeth's mom.

She tried to enlarge the images to see more details. But it was no use. The camera wasn't high quality enough.

"Does that help at all?" Rebecca propped her hip against the doorway and crossed her arms as she watched Cassidy work.

"I'll need a copy of this video footage," Cassidy said. "I'd like to keep it in my files. Looking at the video, I can't say anything definitively."

Rebecca shivered and rubbed the side of her arms. "I don't know what's going on, but I don't like it."

"Neither do I." Cassidy leaned back in the leather office chair and turned to Rebecca. "Can you tell me, based on your records, when this reservation was made?"

"Absolutely." As Rebecca rushed toward her computer, Cassidy rose, allowing her to sit down and type.

A few minutes later, Rebecca said, "Mrs. Manchester made a last-minute partial week reservation just four days ago."

Cassidy narrowed her gaze. "Is that unusual?"

"It is. We don't usually do partial weeks. But if someone is willing to pay all the fees associated with the full week while only staying for half a week, then we'll let them, at the owner's discretion."

"Is there anything else in your notes about the reservation?"

Rebecca leaned closer to the screen. "Not really. It says Mrs. Manchester came from Raleigh."

The location fit also. Cassidy made a mental note

of that fact. "So Mrs. Manchester made a reservation four days ago and then checked in when?"

"Three days ago." Rebecca shivered again.

But the question remained . . . why had the culprit waited until this morning to call about checkout? The rental agreement would have ended soon anyway. Why not just wait for the cleaners to show up when the partial rental was over? Why call the departure in at all?

The more Cassidy thought this through, the more questions she had.

She stared at the video footage on the screen again and frowned. If Alexandria was the one who'd been attacked in that house, then there was little hope she was alive. There was just too much blood.

Cassidy's stomach twisted into a knot at the thought . . . especially when she thought about Annabeth.

CASSIDY WAS NOWHERE NEAR FINISHED for the day. She had evidence to file, reports to write up, and phone calls to make.

But first, she had to see Ty and Annabeth. She

needed to talk to Ty, and there were some conversations that shouldn't be had over the phone.

Kujo, their golden retriever, greeted Cassidy at the door. She rewarded the canine with a hearty head rub.

As soon as Cassidy closed the door behind her, Ty stepped from the kitchen.

The former Navy SEAL always had an ear for trouble—or *potential* trouble. Very little got past him.

Even better, not only was Ty tough, but he was also tender. He was patient with Annabeth. He cooked and cleaned as an equal partner in their relationship. And he let Cassidy take charge in her investigations, just as she'd been hired to do, instead of feeling the need to feed his macho side.

Cassidy knew not every man was like him, though. She thanked God every day that He'd brought Ty into her life. Ty was just the person she needed, and he'd been there for her on her worst days—and she'd had plenty of those.

"What's wrong?" Ty seemed to pick up on the dark cloud hanging over her.

He stepped closer, his gaze assessing her. His dark hair had been haphazardly brushed away from his face, and he needed to shave—though Cassidy kind of liked the scruffy look sometimes. He even had a dishtowel draped over his shoulder, a look Cassidy found surprisingly attractive.

Cassidy glanced behind him, trying to choose her words wisely. Privacy was essential right now. "Where's Annabeth?"

"She fell asleep while watching cartoons in the bedroom. What's going on?"

"I don't have much time." She shifted, resting her hand on her duty belt. "But there are a couple of developments I didn't want to tell you about over the phone."

Concern flashed in Ty's gaze. "You've got my attention."

Cassidy filled him in on the crime scene and the fact that Alexandria Manchester had potentially rented the space.

Ty ran a hand over his face, tension rippling through his posture. "That's one plot twist I didn't expect."

"You and me both." Cassidy frowned, hesitantly drawing her gaze up to his. "But there's more."

She didn't want to tell him the rest. Didn't want to concern him. Didn't want Ty to take on any more burdens than he already had.

But Cassidy couldn't keep this update to herself. Doing so wouldn't be fair.

That same concern stained the depths of Ty's blue eyes as he patiently waited for her to continue. "Go on."

"I got a phone call." Cassidy's throat burned as she said the words, and she lowered her voice, even though she knew nobody else was around. "Someone said, 'we know who you are.'"

"We know who you are?"

She nodded. "That's all this man said before the line went dead."

Ty's eyes narrowed. "Did you try to trace the call?"

"No, but I will as soon as I get back to the station. I'm quite certain it came from a burner phone. Even not-so-smart criminals know not to use their own phones."

"Do you think . . . ?" Ty paused, almost as if he couldn't finish the statement. Instead, he rubbed his throat.

"The world thinks that Cady Matthews is dead." Cassidy used every ounce of her strength to control the tremble in her voice so Ty wouldn't hear her fear. "That fact is the only reason I've been able to live with any kind of peace for the past couple of years. But I've always known there was a possibility someone might find out I didn't really die that day. And if that's the case . . ."

Ty wrapped his arms around her in a bear hug. Cassidy leaned into her husband, grateful for his strength. If she let herself, she might lose it and fall to pieces right now.

That's why she couldn't let herself go there.

"We don't know anything for sure," Ty murmured in her ear.

"No, we don't. But . . ."

"We'll be vigilant until we have more information. But we can't make any snap decisions. Okay?"

Cassidy nodded against his chest, his logic making perfect sense. "You're right. That's what we should do. But I wanted to come home and tell you myself."

Ty leaned back, leaving his hands resting between Cassidy's neck and shoulders as he gazed into her eyes. "What can I do for you, sweetheart?"

She drew in a deep breath, still trying to hold herself together.

"Just keep an eye on Annabeth. I can take care of myself." Even as Cassidy said the words, she knew they weren't entirely true.

To an extent, yes, Cassidy could take care of herself. She was a trained law enforcement professional. But no man was an island, as the saying went. And if the ruthless members of the deadly gang who'd had a bounty on Cassidy's head found her in Lantern Beach, it would be a battle until the bloody end.

Because Cassidy, while undercover and in a struggle for her life, had killed their esteemed leader.

In the eyes of his loyal followers, that was a crime punishable by death.

Cassidy thought she'd escaped from the danger.

But was escape truly even possible?

Nausea gurgled in her stomach at the thought.

CHAPTER FOUR

AFTER CASSIDY LEFT to go back to work, Ty's thoughts remained on her words. He tried to keep himself occupied as he and Annabeth made cookies together. But his mind kept wandering back to the message she'd received.

We know who you are.

What if somebody really *had* discovered Cassidy's true identity?

That development would change everything.

Ty and Cassidy had built a nice life for themselves in Lantern Beach. But before they'd ever gotten married, Ty had known about Cassidy's past. He'd known the risks.

And he would marry her all over again. He had no regrets.

However, the thought of everything being turned upside down made his chest tighten.

Ty had spent countless hours building his dream of opening Hope House and then he'd later formed Blackout. Hope House was a retreat program for injured veterans, and Blackout was a private security firm that employed former Special Forces.

He felt he'd been called to Lantern Beach, that it was the ideal location for both organizations.

Now everything might be on the precipice of changing.

But even more than that, there was Cassidy. The idea of anything happening to her . . . Ty couldn't even stomach the thought.

He glanced at Annabeth as she stirred some chocolate chips into the dough. He smiled when he saw her tongue poking out of her mouth as she concentrated on mixing everything together in the bowl.

The two of them had bonded over the past week. Not only did they conquer jigsaw puzzles and play board games and color pictures together, but they'd also gone on walks and played with Kujo.

Sure, Ty had other things he had to do. But he got them done as needed. Sometimes, his and

Cassidy's friends came over to help with Annabeth. Any way Ty looked at it, everything had worked out.

He was so glad to have the girl here with them. Ty didn't like the fact Annabeth had already been through so much, and he was determined to protect her from anything else that might go wrong. At least, he would do everything in his power to keep her safe.

Kujo suddenly stood from where he'd been lying near the fireplace and barked. Instantly, Ty's muscles tightened.

He glanced at the door and saw a shadow on the other side of the curtain covering the window.

Who was here?

He wasn't expecting anyone, and his friends knew to text before showing up. It had become the new rule since Annabeth arrived.

"Annabeth, go to your room for a minute. Take Kujo."

The girl's eyes widened as she stared at him. She must have heard the urgency in his voice because she dropped the wooden spoon back into the bowl.

She then scrambled toward Kujo, took his collar, and hurried down the hallway. Ty waited until he heard her door click shut before glancing back at the front of the house again.

Ty pulled his gun from the holster at his waist. He made sure to keep the weapon on him, especially now with all of this going on.

Maybe he was paranoid. But he couldn't take any chances. The stakes were too high.

Ty gripped his gun as he stepped closer to the door.

He was about to find out.

CAUTIOUSLY, Ty opened the door.

A man he'd never seen before stood on the other side.

The sixty-something male had a full salt-and-pepper beard and matching hair. He wore a white polo shirt with some type of logo on it and held a leather bag at his side.

The man offered a wide grin. "I hope I'm not catching you at a bad time."

Ty kept his gun beside him, hidden behind the door as to not alert the man if it wasn't necessary. "Can I help you?"

"I'm Rob, and I noticed your windows have some moisture between the panes. Have you ever thought about replacing them?"

This guy was a salesman?

That's when the words on the logo of the man's polo shirt came into focus. *True View Windows.*

Ty's shoulders remained tight. "We don't get many solicitors around here, not with so many rental properties and so few permanent residents."

In all of Ty's years living here, this was one of the only times he remembered *ever* getting a solicitor, for that matter.

"My company has just started servicing houses in this area, so I'm trying to drum up some new business." The man shrugged. "What can I say? I've always been called a go-getter."

Ty shook his head. This man's timing couldn't be worse. "We're not interested in new windows at this time. Sorry."

"I understand. But here's a brochure just in case you change your mind." The man handed him something.

Ty glanced at the trifold a moment before taking it from the man.

Then he watched the man walk away before closing the door and locking it. Ty walked to the window and peered outside. Rob got into a truck with the same logo from his T-shirt plastered on the side of the door.

As the man pulled away, Ty looked down at the advertisement. It appeared that was all the glossy trifold was. A piece of paper. Information. No hidden dangers.

Ty nearly laughed.

There he went, looking for something suspicious even in the most innocent moment.

He tucked away the brochure before going to get Annabeth.

He needed to make sure the girl knew everything was okay.

And then they needed to bake these cookies.

CHAPTER FIVE

AFTER SHE LEFT HER HOUSE, Cassidy headed back to the crime scene. She needed to see it again with her own eyes, to conduct a secondary survey.

It was nearly six o'clock in early May, which meant the sun was sinking lower on the horizon as twilight began. Cassidy still had a couple of hours until darkness would fully consume the sky.

Cassidy stood at the back of the living room and took several deep breaths, willing herself to relax. She hadn't felt this worked up in a long time, like her insides were a frenzied mess that she couldn't tame. That caller had really thrown her off-kilter.

Banks still stood guard outside, providing an extra layer of protection as she gave all her time and energy to piecing together the story of what had happened here.

Cassidy closed her eyes. *I could use Your help right now, God. Someone needs justice here. Help me find these answers.*

When she opened her eyes again, a focused sense of calm washed over her.

Her gaze went to the kitchen wall. The blood pattern indicated cast-off rather than gunshot spatter.

If Cassidy had to guess, the victim had been stabbed.

Cassidy imagined Alexandria in the kitchen. Had she been cooking or getting her morning coffee when a stranger surprised her?

She studied the kitchen counter.

It was clear, with no signs of coffee or any other beverages or food.

She sucked on her bottom lip, still trying to visualize the scene.

The crime had probably taken place in the dark. In the daytime, too many people would have been around.

Maybe the victim had been making a phone call and staring out the window when she'd heard a footstep behind her.

The blood all over the front section of the house indicated a fight had ensued. If Cassidy had to guess, the struggle had started in the kitchen but had moved into the living room. That was where the victim had most likely spent his or her final moments.

A large pool of blood had dried there on the floor. Based on the relatively clean area rug, the victim had been carried away from the scene from that spot.

Cassidy closed her eyes again.

She imagined the killer pulling out a tarp. Did he run out to the car to get it?

Maybe.

She pictured him laying the blue plastic on the floor near the victim. Lifting her. Placing her on it. Wrapping her up tight.

The murderer had then carried the victim out to his vehicle—that would explain why there was no blood evidence to follow outside of these four walls. He would have taken her somewhere to dispose of her.

But why? Why not leave her here?

Unless this person didn't want people to know who she was.

Was that because the woman who'd been

staying here wasn't Alexandria Manchester? Had someone set this up to make people think it was her?

Or maybe the victim really was Alexandria, but someone didn't want people to discover her true identity.

But someone that meticulous would have known that Alexandria's name was on record at the rental agency.

The questions whirled in Cassidy's head.

She didn't have any more answers now than she'd had before.

But at least she had a theory about what had happened here.

Right now, she was going to go talk to some neighbors. Maybe someone had seen or heard something.

CASSIDY STEPPED from the cottage and locked the door behind her. Banks looked rigid as he kept guard on the small wooden deck outside.

He barely glanced at her, instead keeping his gaze focused on his surroundings as he addressed her. "Everything okay?"

"I was just trying to get a feel for what happened in there."

"It's stuff like that I don't want to think about." His jaw twitched. "Scenes like that . . . you never forget, do you?"

"Unfortunately, no." Cassidy scanned the outside of the cottage again.

Most of the ground was sandy, dotted with clumps of coarse grass. They'd already gone through the trashcan and looked for any evidence that could have been left outside. They hadn't found anything of note.

Cassidy had left a few tasks for Banks also.

"Did you check for tire prints?" she asked.

"I examined the driveway, looking for anything that might have been left. I took a couple of photos. However, the tracks could be from the victim's car. Either way, I documented them."

She glanced around again. "I'm going to question the neighbors and find out if anyone saw or heard anything. But I'd like you to remain here and guard the scene."

"Whatever you need, Chief."

"Thanks, Banks." She patted his arm as she walked past.

No one was home at the first house, so Cassidy

headed across the street to a cottage with a sedan in the driveway. A man in his fifties answered the door.

He was short and overweight, and reminded Cassidy somewhat of George Costanza from *Seinfeld*. The scents of fried fish and overbearing flowery candles drifted through the open door as he stared at her, his eyes twitching as if he were nervous.

Sometimes, cops had that effect on people.

"I'm sorry to bother you," Cassidy started. "I'm Police Chief Cassidy Chambers."

He nodded. "Chief, I'm Steve. Steve Ricks. Is everything okay?"

"I'm conducting an investigation concerning a crime in this area. I wondered if you'd seen anything strange at the house across the street."

He followed her gaze and pushed his wire-framed glasses up higher on his nose. "That one?"

Cassidy glanced back at the cottage where Banks stood. "Yes, that's the one."

He pursed his lips in thought, his actions jerky and quick. "I saw a woman pull up a few days ago. She grabbed her bag and headed inside. I didn't see her after that."

"Can you describe her car?"

He shrugged. "I think it was a blue sedan. I wasn't paying much attention. I'm sorry."

"Did anybody else pull up while you were here? Were there any other signs of life at the house?"

His shoulders lurched up before softening again. "I saw two ladies drive up this morning. Then police cars came a few minutes later. But that's it. The only time I ever notice anything happening over there is when I eat. My dining room window overlooks that house. Besides, I didn't come here to spy on my neighbors. I came here to relax."

This conversation had gotten her nowhere. But Cassidy hadn't been expecting much.

"Thank you for your help." Cassidy handed him her card. "If you think of anything else, give me a call."

Cassidy made her way to the other houses, but she only heard more of the same.

It looked like the woman who'd been staying at the house had mostly remained inside and to herself.

Interviewing the neighbors had only led to a dead end.

Cassidy paused at her SUV and frowned.

Someone somewhere had to have some answers.

But the tricky part was finding that person.

Just then, imaginary spiders crawled up Cassidy's spine.

She slowly scanned the area around her.

Was someone watching her?

Her instincts told her they were.

She continued looking around.

Banks still stood by the door, but he stared straight ahead, reminding Cassidy of one of the guards at Kensington Palace.

It wasn't him.

She looked at the house beside this one and the woods surrounding it. Then the road. And the next house. And the next.

And then—

As Cassidy turned toward the house where Steve was staying, the curtain dropped.

She sucked in a breath.

Was the man hiding something? Was he nervous? Or just nosy?

Cassidy didn't know.

But she'd need to keep that question in the back of her mind.

CHAPTER SIX

<hr>

BACK AT THE CRIME SCENE, Cassidy called Officer Dane Bradshaw and asked him to meet her with his canine. Ranger was a German Shepherd mix and a great police dog—the first one they'd had in the Lantern Beach Police Department.

The two of them showed up ten minutes later, and Cassidy met them in the driveway.

Bradshaw was tall with broad shoulders, an olive complexion, and a friendly smile. He'd been one of Cassidy's first hires when she'd taken over as police chief, and he'd proven himself to be an asset here in Lantern Beach.

Cassidy turned away from the breeze, which had picked up over the past hour. She pushed a few stray hairs from her face as she addressed her officer.

"I worked a case back in—" Cassidy had almost said Seattle but stopped herself. "I mean, I *read about* a case back in Virginia where a police dog was able to follow the scent of a body all the way down the road."

How had she almost made that slipup? Cassidy was more careful than that. That phone call today had thrown her off her game. She had to be more on guard.

"Dogs have amazing noses," Bradshaw confirmed.

Cassidy explained what she'd like for them to do. "What do you think?"

Bradshaw rubbed his dog's head as the canine sat at attention beside him. "I say it's worth a shot. But it's getting dark, so we probably need to work fast."

Cassidy wasted no time letting Banks know what was going on and then bringing out a pillow from inside. She'd placed it in a plastic bag, careful to use gloves so she wouldn't contaminate the scent.

Ranger sniffed the fabric, and then Bradshaw bent low, talking in quiet tones to the canine.

A moment later, Ranger's nose went to the driveway. Bradshaw kept hold of the dog's leash and followed behind as the canine started to lead them away from the cottage.

Her heart skipped a beat. Did they actually have a lead? She hadn't expected Ranger to act so quickly. Was she ready for the possible outcome?

The desire to find answers and the fear of where those answers might lead battled inside her.

Because if Alexandria was dead . . . Cassidy didn't know how she would break that news to Annabeth. She didn't even want to think about it.

Cassidy had no choice but to proceed. She *had* to figure out what had happened in the cottage. It was her sworn duty.

Ranger moved at a quick clip down the lane, his nose still to the ground. He was obviously on the trail of something.

But exactly where would the dog lead them?

Cassidy quickened her steps to keep up with them.

The canine continued until he reached the highway cutting through the center of the island. Traffic wasn't heavy at this time of year, but the trio would still need to be careful.

As they headed down the road, Cassidy put a call in to Officer Dillinger and asked him to meet them. For safety purposes, they needed someone to trail behind them. Dillinger had been working at the station, scanning security videos from the ferry to see if he could identify anyone who looked like Alexandria Manchester arriving.

No bridges led to the island. Only the ferry or private charters allowed people to come and go from this secluded stretch of sand.

"Good job, boy," Bradshaw muttered in front of her. "Keep going."

Ranger didn't need encouragement. His nose remained to the ground, and he kept following the scent.

But as Cassidy turned around, she spotted a car coming toward them.

She waved her hands in the air, urging the driver to slow.

Instead, the vehicle almost seemed to pick up speed.

She drew in a quick breath as her adrenaline kicked in.

"Bradshaw . . ." Cassidy's voice held an edge of warning.

"What's wrong?" Bradshaw continued forward, not looking back.

"The car coming toward us isn't slowing." Cassidy held her breath, preparing herself to act.

She waved her hands in the air again, hoping to get the driver's attention.

But nothing changed.

Was the driver charging at them on purpose?

That was the only explanation that made sense.

"Chief . . . ?" Bradshaw called over his shoulder.

Cassidy quickly glanced back at her officer and his canine.

She didn't want Ranger to lose the scent . . .

But when she looked at the oncoming car again, it continued to barrel toward them.

If they didn't act soon, the vehicle would collide into them in less than twenty seconds.

"Bradshaw!" Cassidy yelled. "Look out!"

She darted from the asphalt and launched across a ditch. Cassidy landed hard on her knees and elbows as the driver accelerated and sped past them.

Cassidy's heart pounded against her chest as she watched the fleeing vehicle.

The windows were tinted. She couldn't see who was inside.

But she was able to get a partial plate.

She glanced across the grass at Bradshaw and Ranger. Bradshaw had dived onto the ground beside her, and Ranger stood between them, eyeballing the retreating car as if he sensed the danger they'd been in.

"Are you two okay?" Cassidy called.

Bradshaw pulled himself to his feet then checked out Ranger.

"We're fine. But that was too close." His gaze narrowed with anger as he glanced at the road.

As the vehicle disappeared from sight, Cassidy pulled out her phone and called Dillinger to find out his approximate location. He was still a few minutes away.

Cassidy frowned.

There was no way she could catch that sedan on foot.

Exactly what was going on?

Whatever it was, this wasn't the end. Whoever was responsible for the scene at that house obviously had more devious acts planned. More messages to send. More crimes to cover up.

That thought did not settle well with Cassidy.

CASSIDY FOLLOWED behind Bradshaw and Ranger as they headed down the highway again. She'd opened the bag with the pillowcase and let

Ranger sniff inside. He'd picked up right where he'd left off.

Dillinger had pulled behind them and now escorted them as Ranger followed the scent. No one should try to run them off the road again.

Cassidy ignored the ache in her elbows and knees—but she couldn't ignore what had just almost happened. Someone had wanted to send a clear message, a message that danger still lurked here on the island.

Anger turned Cassidy's blood hot when she thought about it.

Most likely, the person behind the steering wheel was the same person who was responsible for whatever had happened at that crime scene.

He was still on this island.

And Cassidy planned on finding him.

Ranger barked before pausing by a gravel road.

"What is it, boy?" Bradshaw asked in soothing tones.

Cassidy held her breath as she waited to see what the canine would do.

After another moment of sniffing, Ranger turned down the lane. The narrow street led away from the ocean and toward the Pamlico Sound. Cassidy had been down this way before and knew there were clusters of aging fishing cabins in this area.

The dog slowed halfway down the road.

Was the scent growing fainter?

Cassidy's steps faltered also. After a moment, the dog continued down the secluded road. Dillinger remained behind them.

"You're doing good, boy," Bradshaw murmured.

As they got closer to the end of the lane, Cassidy saw the sparkling water in the distance.

The Pamlico Sound.

The setting sun cast an orange glow over everything around it, practically making the water look as if it were on fire.

A one-story cottage rose near the water's edge. The place was one of the older ones on the island. Rugged and weathered. Not well-kept. From all appearances, it looked like no one had cared for the place in a very long time.

The hurricane shutters had been pulled over the windows. Trash clustered beneath the stilts of the house. Crab pots had been left haphazardly, each one rusting. One of the steps leading up to the front door was broken.

Could the killer be squatting here? It was worth checking out.

After Cassidy figured out where the dog was leading them.

Ranger stopped at a sandy area near the water.

Then he sat and sniffed the air.

Bradshaw frowned. "It looks like he lost the scent."

Cassidy's hands went to her hips as she paused for a moment. "Or maybe someone put the body in a boat and left the island."

"It's a real possibility."

Just as she glanced away from the water, a sound split the air.

It almost sounded like a bang.

And the noise had come from inside the cottage beside them.

Cassidy reached for her weapon as she started toward the seemingly deserted structure.

CHAPTER SEVEN

WITH DILLINGER BY HER SIDE, Cassidy cautiously approached the house.

The dog's scent hadn't led them to this cottage. But that didn't mean there wasn't reason to be concerned right now.

Quietly, Cassidy and Dillinger climbed the rickety steps to the cottage.

As they reached the porch, birds rushed from behind the eaves.

The sudden motion caused Cassidy's pulse to surge.

Birds. Just birds, she reminded herself.

Still, her heart pounded at a quick clip in her chest.

As they stepped closer, the scent of decay rose

around them. Cassidy wasn't sure what she'd find inside this place. But she needed to be prepared for anything.

Still gripping her gun, she stood on one side of the door and Dillinger the other. She nodded to her officer before throwing the door open.

"Police!" she yelled.

She and Dillinger barged inside.

Cassidy paused in the entry and glanced around the dark space, waiting for her eyes to adjust to the dimness.

Piles of junk filled the floor. Old magazines. Boxes. Electronics.

Everything felt frozen with silence.

The only movement was the disturbed dust particles floating through the air.

The scent of rot became stronger as Cassidy stepped deeper into the house.

As she glanced across the room, she spotted a hole in the wall. Pine straw and dry grass protruded from it. It was a nest of some sort, Cassidy realized.

Nature had taken residence here, which explained some of the smell. This place would be perfect shelter for birds, raccoons, and mice. She kept that detail in the back of her mind.

Carefully, Cassidy continued forward.

Three doorways waited in front of them.

If someone was inside this place, they could be behind any one of those doors.

She and Dillinger headed toward the hallway together, weapons ready for action if necessary.

Cassidy reached the first door, turned the knob, and gently pushed it open. Cautiously, she stepped inside and glanced around.

An old bedroom stared back. The room was stacked full of junk just like the rest of the place. The closet doors were gone and revealed a wall of boxes.

Nobody was in here.

Dillinger checked the room across the hall and gave her a nod to indicate it was clear also.

Together, they headed toward the room at the end of the hallway.

When they both lined either side, Cassidy nodded at Dillinger.

He threw the door open.

An avocado-colored bathroom greeted them.

An *empty* avocado-colored bathroom.

"Looks like no one's been here in a long time," Cassidy muttered, feeling a strange mix of disappointment and relief.

"That's how it appears."

Placing her gun back into her holster, Cassidy

turned to Dillinger. "You heard it too, right? The bang?"

Dillinger nodded, his face still tense as if he didn't want to let down his guard. "I did. I don't know what it could have been."

As they walked back into the living area, Cassidy glanced around.

She was missing something. But what?

Just as that thought crossed her mind, something —or someone—sprang in front of her.

CASSIDY REACHED FOR HER WEAPON, ready to act.

But instead, a cat arched his back and sent Cassidy an annoyed hiss.

The black feline regarded Cassidy a moment before letting out a loud meow and sashaying away.

Cassidy released her breath and holstered her weapon. "A cat."

Dillinger chuckled and shook his head. "Better than an armed man."

"I can't disagree with that," Cassidy muttered. "Now I understand the smell. The cat's probably feral."

"Where there's one feral cat, there's usually a whole colony."

As if the cats had understood what Dillinger said, two more suddenly appeared. The felines must have been hiding behind some boxes or in a cabinet.

Cassidy stepped into the kitchen. When she did, she spotted a box of books on the floor and a rectangular outline in the dust on the table.

Realization dawned on her.

One of the cats must have knocked a box onto the floor.

That was the sound they'd heard.

"It looks like we found our culprit." Cassidy picked up an old Stephen King hardback and showed her officer.

Dillinger shook his head again. "I guess this has led us nowhere?"

Cassidy thought about the dog and about the water.

In some ways, the clues hadn't given them answers. But at least they now knew that the perp had most likely put his victim on a boat.

Cassidy remembered when the Shacklefords had been on the island and she'd been pursuing them.

At one point, the couple had abandoned their vehicle for a boat.

Could those two really be behind this?

And if that was the case, where was their vehicle now? They obviously hadn't left it here near this fishing cottage.

Could one of them be staying behind? Had either Lars or Emma been in that car that had tried to run them down?

It was a good possibility that at least one of them remained here on the island.

If so, Cassidy was going to find them.

Everything that was important to her depended on it.

CHAPTER EIGHT

"CHIEF, you're going to want to see this." Bradshaw stood outside the cottage, waiting for her with Ranger at his side.

Cassidy's curiosity spiked as she and Dillinger followed Bradshaw down the lane.

He paused near the edge of the woods and pointed to the ground. "Tread marks."

Cassidy squatted to get a better look.

Sure enough, Bradshaw was right. Tires had left a distinct pattern on some wet dirt at the edge of the trees.

"We're going to need to take an impression of these and see if they match the treads found at the cottage." Even as Cassidy said the words, she knew that the two would most likely match.

Ranger hadn't let them down before, and he wasn't going to let them down today.

"I can do that," Dillinger volunteered. "I have a kit in my car."

As Dillinger walked away, Cassidy rubbed Ranger's head again. "You're a smart boy."

The dog leaned into her touch, his tongue happily hanging from his mouth as if he were proud of himself too.

Cassidy glanced up at her officer. "You too, Bradshaw. Good job."

"I know who the star of this show is." Bradshaw grinned. "I'm happy we could help. I just want to catch the person who's behind this and find our victim. Do you think there's any hope this person is still alive?"

Cassidy wished she could be optimistic in this situation. But she shook her head. "Based on the amount of blood at that scene, I don't see how."

Any amusement left Bradshaw's gaze. "So as far as you're concerned, this is a murder we're investigating, not a missing person?"

"That's correct. I'm going to let other law enforcement offices in this area know what's going on here. Although I suspect whoever did this is still on the island—or at least one of them is—they could be long gone by now. Until we know for sure, we need to spread the word."

"Understood. If there's anything else Ranger can help with, let me know."

Cassidy nodded and waited for Dillinger to finish taking a cast of that tire tread. Then she needed him to drive them back to the cottage to pick up their vehicles. Because they still had a lot of work to do.

TY TUCKED Annabeth into bed before heading back into the living room.

What a day.

After making a fire to ward away the slight chill in the air, Ty lowered himself onto the couch and rubbed Kujo's head. Benjamin James, one of the Blackout agents, stood guard outside of the house tonight.

It brought Ty a measure of comfort to know he had extra sets of eyes around.

But there was no way he could relax, not with everything that was going on.

For Annabeth's sake, Ty tried to make sure things remained normal here at the house. But his mind had been on everything Cassidy had told him.

Trouble seemed to be attracted to this island. Not *just* trouble—but trouble and good times both. The dichotomy could be dizzying at times.

So many people came to Lantern Beach to be refreshed. To spend time with family. To get away from everyday life.

But on the other side of the coin, there were also people who came to this island because it was isolated. Secluded. Off the beaten path.

Then there were those who came here for a purpose—purposes like hunting down people as a matter of vengeance.

Ty's stomach clenched at the thought of it.

He picked up a cookie he and Annabeth had made. The place still smelled like vanilla, sea salt, and a crackling fireplace. They were normally some of Ty's favorite scents.

But enjoying himself at a time like this seemed irreverent.

Ty had spent his summers on the island as a child, and he'd always thought of this as a little slice of heaven. As he'd gotten older, he realized this place was far from perfect—but it *was* special.

His phone buzzed, and he glanced at the screen,

hoping to see a message from Cassidy. Though she worked late sometimes, Ty still hoped that she might come home at a relatively decent hour tonight.

But he didn't recognize the number on his screen.

He clicked on the message anyway.

When he did, his eyes widened.

Someone had sent him some photos.

He clicked on one, noticing the beach in the background on the thumbnail.

But it wasn't until Ty enlarged the image that he noticed that he, Annabeth, and Kujo were also in that picture.

Based on the shirt that Ty wore, the photo had been taken earlier today when the three of them had taken a walk.

His gut tightened.

Someone had been watching them.

Ty had been careful, had looked around to make sure danger wasn't lurking nearby.

Yet it had been.

Lava filled his veins at the thought of it.

He studied the angles of the photos. They appeared to have been taken from far away using a telephoto lens.

Someone wanted to make it known who was calling the shots, who was in charge.

But Ty wouldn't let this person get the best of him.

There was no way he would let someone else win.

Especially not when Cassidy and Annabeth were the ones in the crosshairs.

CHAPTER NINE

CASSIDY ESCAPED to her office bright and early the next morning. It was just as well that she'd given up on rest and gone into work.

She couldn't sleep last night anyway, not with all the thoughts rushing through her head—starting with the fact that Ty had been sent those photos.

Someone was clearly sending a message, and Cassidy didn't like it.

The threats stoked the fire inside her even more —the fire to find answers, to bring justice to the person who was sending them.

First, she'd run the plate of the car that had almost run her and Bradshaw—and Ranger—down.

The vehicle had been stolen from Nags Head, a town located a good two hours from Lantern Beach.

She had a feeling that particular lead would go nowhere. These people were too smart for that.

Next, she dug deeper into the Shacklefords.

The couple had once worked for the CIA. But apparently, they'd been fired. Afterward, they'd become professional hitmen.

Just last week, the two of them had come into the station pretending to be a couple by the name of the Donovans. They'd said that their daughter Annabeth had jumped into the water while they were boating during a storm. When Cassidy had tried to confirm their IDs, they'd escaped, knowing that Cassidy would figure out they weren't who they said.

In the time since then, Cassidy had learned that the pair was truly deadly. They had a long list of hits they'd made and crimes they'd committed.

They had been hired by a man named Richard Robertson to help abduct Joe and Alexandria Manchester, Annabeth's parents. Robertson had wanted to use Joe Manchester as part of his plan to take down the North Carolina governor and ensure he suffered in the process.

That led Cassidy to conclude that the Shacklefords still might have Alexandria.

But why would they hold onto Alexandria after the job was done? And if they really had held onto her, had she gotten away and come to Lantern Beach to rent that house? If so, why hadn't she come forward to claim Annabeth as soon as she arrived?

The questions confounded Cassidy until her head began to throb.

She wasn't ready yet to say definitively that Alexandria was the one who'd been killed. Maybe that defied logic on some levels, but she didn't feel sure yet.

She hoped law enforcement from another town would know something.

Meanwhile, Cassidy sat at her desk writing her reports. Doing so helped her to sort out everything that had happened. But until she had more information, it would be impossible to begin drawing any types of conclusions.

As she stared at all the facts in front of her, a knock sounded at her door.

She looked up and saw Paige Henderson, her dispatcher and receptionist, standing there. Based on the look on her face, she wasn't very happy.

"Some men are here to see you," she said.

Cassidy's spine straightened at the ominous tone in her voice. "Who?"

Paige frowned before saying, "The FBI."

"WHAT CAN I HELP YOU WITH?"

Cassidy stared at the FBI agent sitting across from her in her office. He'd introduced himself as Special Agent Donald Watkins from the Raleigh field office. Two of his colleagues stood stiffly behind him.

Watkins had a square face, light brown hair cut short, and intense blue eyes. Cassidy would guess him to be in his early forties. He wore cologne so strong that it nearly created a hedge of protection around him.

"Let me get straight to the point," he started. "We heard you have a crime scene with no victim."

"We do." She was surprised that word of that had reached the FBI, however.

"We monitor what's going on at various police precincts in our district," he explained as if he had anticipated her unspoken question.

"So what has you so interested about this case?" Cassidy laced her fingers together as she waited to hear his answer. The FBI didn't usually get involved in situations like these.

"I'm afraid I can't discuss all the details. But we need to see the scene."

"Of course. It sounds like this could be a matter of a federal investigation," Cassidy said, but she couldn't imagine why.

She wasn't sure what kind of information she was going to get from this man. But if three FBI agents had come all the way out here to see the scene, this must be a big deal.

"We aren't saying that this will become our case," Watkins said each of his words slowly, carefully. "We're still looking into things."

She knew they wouldn't answer any more of her questions right now, so she nodded. "I can take you to see it."

"Perfect. We'll follow you there."

"Sounds like a plan." Cassidy grabbed her keys and stood.

She remained calm on the outside. But inside her thoughts rushed and churned like the ocean during a hurricane. She desperately wanted to know what this was about. Clearly, she was missing something.

She and Watkins made small talk as they walked outside and climbed into their respective vehicles. The other two agents followed Watkins without comment.

As Cassidy headed down the road, she called Mac MacArthur.

Mac was the mayor, but he'd been the police chief here before she came. Today, he was also a mentor and friend.

"If it's not my favorite cop," Mac answered. "What can I do for you, Cassidy?"

Cassidy stared at the road in front of her, grateful for the sunshine and blue skies. She'd enjoy them while she could, especially since they might get a storm in a couple more days. "Sorry to cut to the chase, but have you heard the latest here on the island?"

Mac always knew what was happening on Lantern Beach. He somehow had that ability to sense trouble, almost like birds sensed an incoming storm.

"I did," Mac said. "A bloody cottage with no body. What about it?"

"The FBI just showed up."

He paused before clucking his tongue. "Is that right? Well, it sounds like things are about to get interesting."

"I have no idea why the feds would come here for a case like this." Cassidy explained to Mac that Alexandria Manchester's name was on the rental agreement.

Mac clucked his tongue again. "So you think this ties back in with Annabeth? With Governor Hollick? With Richard Robertson and Buxton Pharmaceuticals?"

If only she knew the answers to those questions.

"As far as we know, the governor was only guilty of trying to profit off his decisions," Cassidy said.

Hollick was still under investigation by authorities for giving government funding to his brother's pharmaceutical company back when Hollick had worked for the National Institutes of Health. Hollick remained in office during the process.

When Hollick had made the call to help his brother's company, he'd taken away funding for a similar project from Buxton Pharmaceuticals. As a result, the president of that company had tried to exact revenge on Hollick.

"Richard Robertson, the president of Buxton Pharm, is now behind bars for his attempt on Hollick's life." Cassidy rehashed the details "And Ty and I have Annabeth."

"This is connected somehow," Mac said. "You know that, right? It has to be."

Cassidy frowned as she gripped the steering

wheel. "That's what my gut's telling me. I just don't know what the connection could be."

"You'll figure it out. Give it time. And if there's one piece of advice I can give you, it's this. Play nice with the FBI—at least to their faces. Behind their backs? It's a fair fight to find answers."

Cassidy smiled. Mac always had the best advice.

"I'll let you know if I need anything," she told him.

"You do that. Have fun."

She ended the call just as she pulled up to Seacret Escape.

Cassidy needed to read between the lines and figure out what was going on here.

CHAPTER TEN

"SO, THIS IS WHERE IT HAPPENED?" Watkins muttered. His partners flanked either side of him and stared at the bloody mess inside Seacret Escape.

"It is." Cassidy kept her voice even and professional. Even though she'd seen this place already, the amount of blood still left her uneasy.

Watkins glanced at her. "Do you know who was staying here?"

"Alexandria Manchester's name was on the rental agreement."

Watkins nodded slowly. "Yet you didn't use her name when you reported this crime?"

"I'm not certain she's the one who was involved with this."

He narrowed his gaze, obviously thinking deeply

about his next words. "I'm going to need you to explain that a little more."

Funny how Cassidy had to explain things, but he didn't. But she remembered Mac's advice to play nice.

Cassidy told him about Annabeth, Annabeth's parents, and Governor Hollick.

Watkins nodded at each new reveal, but his gaze remained strangely aloof and guarded.

He rubbed his chin as he asked, "But you're not sure this girl's mom was the one staying here? Why?"

"It's a long story. But I believe someone might still be holding Alexandria Manchester captive. From all accounts, she's a great mother. If she was free to move about, she would have come to get her daughter. I have no doubt about that."

His gaze narrowed even more. "So why would someone else use her name on the rental agreement?"

"Maybe to send a message? To throw us off their trail?"

Watkins seemed so patient as he processed everything Cassidy told him that she felt like she might climb up a wall. She wanted to see some emotion, for his expression to offer a clue.

But he was too good for that.

"So you think that someone still has Mrs. Manchester and is playing some type of game?" he finally asked, something close to doubt in his voice.

"At this point, that's my best guess. I'm still trying to follow the evidence, of course."

He grunted as if he didn't like that explanation. "Do you have a picture of this Manchester woman?"

"I do." Cassidy pulled out her phone and combed through photos until she found what she was looking for. "Alexandria is married to Joe Manchester, a doctor in Raleigh. She's originally from a town in Northern Virginia. Thirty-three years old. One child."

Cassidy raised her phone so the agents could see her photo.

"Do you mind?" Watkins reached for her phone.

"Not at all." Cassidy gave him the phone and watched him carefully as he stared at the picture.

She didn't get bad vibes from this man. But she *was* curious. Watkins was obviously processing something, formulating ideas. Most likely, he knew something that she didn't.

After studying the photo a moment, he handed her phone back to her. "I'm going to need a copy of this."

"Whatever you need." Cassidy wished that courtesy would be returned to her. But she knew that it wouldn't be.

"Were any personal belongings left behind?" he asked.

"It appears that any personal belongings were burned," Cassidy said. "I collected samples of what I could and sent them off to be tested, along with fingerprints. The challenge with these rental houses is that a lot of people come and go. So I'm not sure what the fingerprints will turn up. I think whoever is responsible for this crime was very careful. The scene was messy, but the cleanup and the removal of the body was meticulous."

Watkins let out another grunt and stared at her a moment before nodding. "I see."

"Are you sure I can't help with anything?" Cassidy already knew what the answer would be.

"Not this time. We'll be taking over this case for you."

Cassidy felt a territorial edge rising up, but she tried to hold the feeling at bay. "What does that mean for me?"

Something flashed in his gaze. Was that dismissal?

Because Cassidy *hated* being dismissed.

"It means that we won't be needing you to investigate." Watkins' voice left no room for argument.

"Will I be kept in the loop?"

He frowned and barely shook his head. "I'm sorry, but this is a matter of national security."

National security?

What in the world was going on?

Cassidy didn't know, and she didn't like it.

AS HE HEARD the front door open, Ty Chambers glanced up from the game of Uno he'd been playing with Annabeth on the coffee table. He'd amended the rules so no talking was required, and now it was Annabeth's favorite.

The tension left Ty's chest when he saw Cassidy step inside.

As he rose from the sofa, so did the girl.

Annabeth's eyes lit up every time she saw Cassidy—and Cassidy's did the same. The two already had quite the bond. Ty sometimes feared what Cassidy's recovery would look like when Annabeth left them one day.

As Cassidy walked across the room, Annabeth

hurried toward her and threw her arms around Cassidy's waist.

A smile spread across Cassidy's face and her skin practically glowed as she hugged the girl back.

She would be a great mom one day.

At the thought, emotion clogged Ty's throat. He prayed Cassidy had that opportunity. They were going through their own little firestorm right now as they tried to handle the news of their infertility.

Cassidy reached up and kissed his cheek. "Hey, hon. How are you?"

"I'd be better if I didn't keep losing the card games we've been playing." He shot Annabeth a knowing look.

The girl smiled.

Annabeth was making progress. When they'd found her just under two weeks ago, not only was the girl mute, but she'd shown very little emotion. Finally, she was at least nodding and giving nonverbal answers.

Ty could only imagine what the girl had been through. He still hoped and prayed that, with time, Annabeth would find her voice again. That she'd be able to tell them the answers they hadn't been able to find on their own. That they'd be able to get her the help she needed.

Ty nodded toward the kitchen. "I wasn't expecting to see you. Can I get you something to eat or drink?"

"A sandwich sounds good," Cassidy said. "Actually, *anything* sounds good right about now."

"You didn't get much sleep again last night."

Ty wasn't trying to lecture Cassidy. But her doctor had stressed how important it was that she take care of herself. And Cassidy always put others in front of herself.

If a case demanded Cassidy's time, then she gave that case her time. Not because she was a workaholic, but because she knew what it was like to need answers, to need closure. She didn't want family and friends of the victims to suffer while not knowing what happened.

That trait made her good at her job.

But it also might be what ultimately led to her demise.

Ty's jaw clenched at the thought.

He snapped his attention back to Cassidy as she sat at the breakfast bar. "Name what you want, and I'll make it for you."

"Really?" She raised her eyebrows. "Anything?"

"As long as we have the ingredients or as long as

you can wait until I run to the store to get the ingredients."

"I'm craving a Philly cheesesteak," she said.

"Craving? That isn't a word you use very often."

"I don't know why," she said. "But a nice crusty hoagie roll with tender beef and gooey cheese is all I've been thinking about."

"I'll see what I can put together for you." Ty knew he had some steak he could slice thin, along with some peppers and onions. He'd do his best to make a sandwich that would make Cassidy proud.

Annabeth climbed up beside her, and Cassidy put an arm around her. The sight of the two of them together warmed his heart.

But Ty also sensed that Cassidy had something she wanted to talk to him about. She tried to be careful not to talk shop too much in front of the girl. Annabeth didn't need to hear about everything going on here.

"Annabeth, can you go look in the upstairs room and see if you can find Kujo's ball?" Ty asked as he pulled out some ingredients. "I think he's ready to play a game of fetch."

The girl nodded, pulled away from Cassidy, and trotted toward the steps.

In some ways, Annabeth seemed so carefree and

happy. Then, in other ways, she seemed haunted. The contrast was jarring.

"What's going on?" Ty turned toward Cassidy, knowing they didn't have a lot of time.

Cassidy lowered her voice. "The FBI is taking over the case."

Ty flinched. "What?"

She filled him in on today's events.

"National security?" Ty continued to slice some steak and peppers as he let those words sink in.

"That's what he said." Cassidy took a long sip of water from her refillable bottle.

Ty paused from prepping the food. "It makes sense, yet it doesn't. Does this have something to do with the governor?"

Cassidy's eyebrows flickered upward. "That's what I wondered as well—although, he's state level, so . . ."

"At least there's one thing we know for sure. Whether or not the victim was Alexandria Manchester, she's somehow involved in this—willingly or not. The fact that her driver's license and name were on the rental agreement says a lot."

Cassidy stared at the cabinet in front of her as if deep in thought. "I agree. Maybe it would serve me well to look into her background a little bit more."

"It couldn't hurt."

Ty finished prepping the food and heated the skillet.

A few minutes later, Annabeth was back with a ball and Kujo. She smiled and giggled as she tossed the tennis ball toward the door and Kujo ran after it.

The sound of a child's laughter in the house was enough to make his heart ache. Home seemed so much warmer when children filled it. Ty had never realized just how true that was until Annabeth came into his life.

Cassidy went over and played with Kujo and Annabeth for a little while until Ty finished her sandwich. But just as he presented it to her on a plate at the breakfast bar, Cassidy's phone rang.

Her eyes lit with a subtle grin when she looked at the screen.

"I know that look," Ty said. "You're up to something."

"I'll explain in a minute." She hit a button on her phone and brought it to her ear.

Ty couldn't wait to hear what was going on.

"THEY'RE HERE," Lisa Dillinger whispered over the phone line. "Just like you thought they might be."

Cassidy tried to ignore the surge of satisfaction she felt. "How many are there?"

"Three."

That was the whole group—at least, it was all Cassidy had seen.

"I seated them near the drink station, and I plan on spending a lot of time there doing refills," Lisa continued, speaking in low tones. "I thought you'd want to know."

Cassidy straightened, things suddenly seeming a little brighter. "You did great, Lisa. I'll come by in a little while."

"Sounds good. In the meantime, I'll keep my ears open."

As Cassidy ended the call, she saw Ty staring at her, curiosity dancing in his eyes.

"What was that about?" Ty leaned with his palms against the counter.

Cassidy plucked a chip from the pile on the plate Ty had set in front of her, but she didn't take a bite. "There aren't a ton of restaurants open here on the island at this time of year. But Lisa's is one of them."

Ty crossed his arms. "So you figured that the FBI agents might go there for lunch?"

Cassidy crunched down on the chip and swallowed before nodding. "Out of the three of them, at least one probably considers himself a foodie. And foodies like Lisa's."

Stereotyping? Yes. But Cassidy had been around enough feds to know their type and be able to peg them more often than not. Today, that had paid off.

Lisa Dillinger owned The Crazy Chefette, a restaurant known for its unique food combinations. It was popular among people looking for food experiences or who liked to try different taste fusions.

"So now you have Lisa doing your dirty work?" Ty tilted his head as he waited for Cassidy's response.

"Dirty work is a bit of an overstatement, don't you think?" Cassidy cast him a skeptical glance. "But I *did* ask Lisa to keep her ears open. You know how people like to get chatty in there. Food does that to people."

"Yes, they do like to get chatty." Ty winked. "Brilliant plan, honey. Just brilliant."

Cassidy grinned. "I try. Now, I'm going to eat my sandwich. Then I need to get to The Crazy Chefette before I miss anything important."

His smile faded. "You do that. But watch your step. Until we know what's going on, everybody needs to be on guard. And we trust no one."

His gaze trailed to Annabeth.

Cassidy glanced at the girl also. She was distracted playing tug-of-war with Kujo.

But Ty's warning pulsed with each of Cassidy's heartbeats. Cassidy wasn't the only one who needed to be careful. So did Ty and Annabeth.

It was anyone's guess at this point what was going on. But if Alexandria Manchester was involved, then there was a good chance that Annabeth was also involved.

Cassidy took the last bite of her sandwich and wiped her mouth. "This was delicious. But I need to go be nosy."

Ty kissed her cheek. "Find some answers. If anyone can figure this out, you can."

———

CASSIDY STEPPED inside The Crazy Chefette and paused a moment as the aroma of fried chicken and sautéed garlic surrounded her. It was a good thing she'd just eaten because the scents teased her taste buds and made her salivate.

A moment later, she spotted the FBI agents in the corner booth and strode toward them. She paused at the front of their table. "Fancy seeing you here."

As Special Agent Watkins looked up at her, something flickered in his gaze. Was that . . . displeasure? The man wasn't happy to see her.

"Small island." He shrugged. "Not many places where we can eat."

"Well, you chose wisely." Cassidy kept her voice friendly. "I hope you got the grilled cheese with peaches. It's a favorite around here."

"Maybe another time." Watkins nodded at his plate. "I decided to get the crab cake instead."

"Another good choice." Cassidy stepped back. "I'll let you all enjoy your food. And, like I said earlier, you let me know if you need anything while you're in town."

"Of course." But Watkins' words sounded stiff and unconvincing.

Cassidy wandered to an empty table on the other side of the restaurant. She wanted to go straight to the back and pepper Lisa with questions. But she knew that might make these guys scrutinize her friend. She didn't want that.

So she would order some lemonade—probably lemonade with jalapeño, another one of Lisa's specialties—and then Cassidy would wait for these guys to leave. Based on what she'd seen of their plates, they were finishing up their meals already.

When she went back to the station, Cassidy needed to look into Alexandria Manchester's background more. There might not be anything there. This might all be a waste of time. But she had to know for certain.

As she watched everyone around her, a man stepped inside—someone she'd never seen before. The man with the salt-and-pepper beard didn't stop and wait to be seated. Instead, he cast a friendly smile to anyone watching before finding his own seat—right beside the FBI agents.

Without a hint of self-consciousness, he picked

up the menu and began browsing it. Cassidy tried to read the logo on his shirt. The man appeared to be a salesman. Maybe replacement windows?

Watkins glanced behind him and scowled, obviously not liking the lack of privacy.

Finally, the FBI agents dropped some cash onto the table and stood. Watkins glanced back at Cassidy as if confirming she was still there. He offered another cordial nod before heading with his crew to the door.

Cassidy waited until their SUV had pulled away before she rose.

She wasted no time in finding Lisa.

She hoped her friend might have overheard something.

And she felt absolutely no shame in her eavesdropping plot.

CHAPTER TWELVE

"THE FEDS WERE A LITTLE TIGHT-LIPPED."
Lisa bounced her baby girl, Julia, on her hip as she
and Cassidy stood in the kitchen speaking in low
tones. In the distance, one of Lisa's sous chefs whis-
tled a tune as he prepared some vegetables.

Cassidy gently ran her thumb over Julia's soft
arm before turning her attention back to Lisa. She
couldn't allow herself to lose her focus right now—
and Julia was an easy distraction. The girl's chubby
thighs were positively adorable.

Cassidy looked at Lisa, forcing herself not to look
at the baby in her friend's arms. "So you didn't hear
anything?"

Satisfaction gleamed in Lisa's eyes. "I didn't say
that."

Cassidy leaned against the counter. She couldn't wait to hear what her friend had to tell her.

"Just as you said, they were talking shop," Lisa started. "They spoke quietly, but I made out a few snippets of their conversation. They kept saying the name Sandra. Does that mean anything to you?"

"Sandra?" Cassidy shook her head. "No, it doesn't ring any bells."

"They said something about Sandra taking off and how they'd pinged her cell phone." Lisa shrugged. "I know it's not much, but I hope that might help you some."

"No, that's great. I don't know exactly where that information will lead, but at least I have a vague idea of what they were talking about."

Maybe this crime scene didn't have anything to do with Alexandria Manchester at all.

But how exactly was Cassidy going to figure out who Sandra was? Without a last name, it would be nearly impossible.

What was the governor's wife's name again? Cassidy thought it was Shirley.

So they weren't talking about the governor. Cassidy would double-check to make sure that nobody else in Hollick's family or on his staff had that name. It *could* be a possibility.

Cassidy shook her head as the mystery continued to deepen.

She was going to get to the bottom of things if it was the last thing she did.

First up on her list: look into Alexandria's background. Next: figure out who Sandra was.

***

CASSIDY LEANED BACK in her desk chair and rubbed her eyes. She'd been staring at the computer screen for the past two hours, trying to learn everything she could about Alexandria Manchester.

Most of what she'd discovered had been exemplary. The woman was married to a doctor. Involved in the community. Had her own successful career as a paralegal.

As Cassidy had gone deeper into the woman's history, she'd reviewed the fact that Alexandria had been a part of the foster-care system as a child.

Cassidy didn't think that had anything to do with the current situation, but she didn't want to overlook anything either.

For someone who'd been in the foster system, Alexandria had done very well for herself—not that being in the foster system ruled out that possibility.

But the trauma that so often led up to being placed in foster care often stuck with kids for life. It always hurt Cassidy's heart to see.

Yet she also knew that didn't always have to be the case. One of the detectives she'd worked with back in Seattle had been in foster care. He'd talked about the counseling he went through and how he'd needed to be brutally honest with himself about the scars he'd been left with. But in the end, he'd made a good life for himself. He was now a great dad and a great husband.

Alexandria's parents had been killed in a convenience store robbery when she was only eleven. Her father had owned his own IT firm, and her mother had been a nurse. She'd had a sickly grandmother who couldn't take care of her. Because of that, she'd been placed in foster care.

Just as Cassidy stood to get herself a cup of coffee, someone knocked at the door.

Paige.

"Chief, I wanted to tell you this in person," Paige said. "We just got a call from Florence, one of the housekeepers with Dream Beach Vacation. She said someone broke into her home and assaulted her."

Cassidy's lungs froze. "Assaulted her?"

"A man burst inside her home to steal some

jewelry, and he got rough with her. She's okay but shaken."

Cassidy let that sink in before shaking her head, trying to get her thoughts straight. "Wait, is this the same Florence that was cleaning the house yesterday where the blood was found?"

Paige's gaze met Cassidy's. "The one and only."

CHAPTER THIRTEEN

CASSIDY SAT with Florence at the woman's dining room table. Florence was a trembling mess.

Cassidy had gotten her some water and now waited for her to calm down some so she could tell Cassidy exactly what happened.

Florence Abram was in her fifties, with a round face and short hair that didn't necessarily flatter her features. She wore an oversized blouse and light-blue jeans. Her cheeks, which always seemed rosy, were now red and splotchy with tears.

She kept grabbing tissues and dabbing her eyes. Every time she did, Cassidy noticed how badly her hands and arms quivered.

Whatever had happened, it had truly shaken her up.

"Take your time," Cassidy encouraged. "Whenever you're ready, you can tell me what happened."

Florence let out an unsteady breath. "Oh, Chief . . . I'm just so . . . I don't even know what to say. I can't believe this happened. I've lived on this island for ten years, and I've never felt unsafe. Even with everything that's happened—and there's been a lot that's happened—I don't even lock my doors at night."

"So what were you doing before all of this began?" Cassidy didn't want to start the questioning in the middle of the action. She needed to start at a moment of normalcy. Maybe that would help get Florence's anxiety under control.

Maybe.

"I was sitting on my couch." Florence picked up a pen and began scribbling on the edge of a piece of paper. "I've also been working on some crossword puzzles. It's my day off so I like to unwind."

"No shame in that."

"I heard a noise at the back of my house." As Florence continued to talk, her muscles seemed to tighten along with her expression. "I thought that maybe I left a window open, and the wind had knocked something down. But then I heard something else.

I don't know why I didn't just leave right then. But it's like I said, I've always felt so safe."

"So what did you do?"

"I got up and went down the hall to see what was happening. But when I opened the door to the bedroom, I saw a man wearing all black standing near my dresser." More tears streamed down her face.

"Could you make out any of his features?"

"He had a mask on, one of those like people wear when they ski."

"So you couldn't tell anything about him?"

Florence shook her head. "No, nothing at all. Except I think maybe he was white. I mean, I could see a little bit of the skin around his eyes."

"You're doing great," Cassidy said. "Go on."

She sucked in several shallow breaths. "I didn't even know what to do when he saw me. I froze. I guess I should have run or looked for a weapon or—"

Cassidy pressed her hand over Florence's arm, trying to reassure her. "It's okay. It happens. People think there's only fight or flight. But a lot of times people freeze. It's perfectly normal."

Florence nodded and ran a trembling hand over

her face. "I didn't know what he was going to do. If he was going to hurt me."

"What was he doing in your bedroom?"

"Looking through my dresser."

Cassidy narrowed her eyes at that bit of news. "Do you have anything of value in your dresser?"

"Not really. As you can see, I don't have a lot." Her gaze swept around her humble home. "I don't make that much as a housekeeper—not even enough to have internet run to the house. But I make enough to live on."

Cassidy shifted, knowing Florence was in a fragile state right now. She didn't want to alarm the woman any more than necessary. "Did this man have anything else in his hands? Anything that he'd taken? Or even anything he brought in with him?"

"I saw a gun in his waistband. That's when I got really scared. I thought he might pull it on me." Her chin trembled.

"What did he do?"

"He asked me where it was. I didn't know what he was talking about. I kept telling him that, but he didn't believe me."

Cassidy could hear the conversation playing out in her mind. "What then?"

"He kept insisting . . . then I remembered one

thing. *Maybe* that was what this guy had come for. I didn't know what else it could be."

"What's that?"

Florence sniffled, her eyes flickering back and forth as she seemed to access her memories. "My mother's engagement ring. I keep it in my sock drawer. I'd wear it myself, but it doesn't fit my fingers. But truly, it's the only thing I have of value, and I don't even think it's *that* valuable. The diamond in it is small."

"How would this guy have known you even had that ring?"

"I mentioned it when I helped work that 5K a couple of weeks ago. Dream Beach sponsored the event, and I worked registration. People won medals, and I brought something up about it. I didn't think much about it. But maybe that was a mistake."

"Did this man take the ring?"

Florence nodded, her eyes welling with more tears. "He asked me where it was, so I pulled it out and gave it to him. Once he had it in his hands, he turned to me. He shoved me out of the way, and I hit the wall. Then he ran out the front door."

"That's not the way he came in though, right?"

"No, the window in my bedroom was raised.

Since my home is one of the few on the island that's not on stilts, it probably wasn't hard to get inside."

Cassidy agreed with that assessment. "Did you hear a car? Or do you think he just ran away?"

"I didn't hear a car. I was so scared at that point that I don't remember much else. I don't remember hearing tires on gravel, so I assume he just ran."

Cassidy leaned closer. "Do you need medical help, Florence?"

Cassidy had already done a quick assessment of the woman. Most of her wounds appeared to be more emotional than physical.

"I don't think so." Florence shook her head. "Like I said, the man just pushed me against the wall. I did hit my head but not hard. It's just the whole situation that has me like this."

Cassidy reached forward and squeezed her arm again. "Can I call someone to come sit with you while I check out the evidence?"

"I'll be fine. Let me just drink my water. I really just want to forget that all of this happened."

AS FLORENCE PRACTICED some controlled breathing, Cassidy searched the woman's place for any evidence that may have been left behind.

Florence told Cassidy that the man had been wearing gloves, so it wasn't surprising when Cassidy didn't find any fingerprints. She'd also searched for fibers on the windowsill and for footprints. She found very little.

She checked the surrounding areas for any tire marks. The only ones at Florence's place belonged to the woman's small, beat-up sedan.

Cassidy ventured into the area surrounding Florence's home and found a small tire print near the woods. She documented that as well, knowing it was a possibility that someone had parked there and then quickly escaped. She'd match it against the prints they'd collected.

Cassidy paused as she stepped back inside Florence's house, taking a deep breath as Florence worked on a crossword puzzle at the table. Cassidy's thoughts raced.

Florence had been one of the people who'd first arrived at the bloody crime scene a couple of days ago. But even if these two crimes were connected, why would someone come to Florence's? Had she seen something before Cassidy had arrived? Was there more to Florence's story?

Cassidy couldn't be certain.

Two hours after the incident, Cassidy was done. Again, Cassidy volunteered to call someone for Florence. But her offer was refused.

Florence was still shaken, but she insisted she wanted to be alone.

With one more glance at Florence, Cassidy departed.

As she stepped outside, she checked her watch and saw it was already after dinnertime.

Though part of her wanted to keep working, Cassidy knew the best thing she could do was to get home. She hadn't slept well last night, and she needed to rest in order to give her best to this case.

And because that's what the doctor had told her she needed to do.

As she paused near her SUV, Cassidy's hand went to her stomach.

She used to imagine her hand resting there because a baby was growing inside. But her doctor had all but dashed their hopes during her last visit.

Now she and Ty had some decisions to make.

And now these new crimes had popped up.

Along with that threat someone had sent her.

We know who you are.

Cassidy still wasn't sure what that was about.

But eventually, she and Ty needed to figure things out.

With that thought in mind, she decided to stop back at the station, drop off the evidence she'd collected, and then get home to spend some time with Ty and Annabeth.

CHAPTER FOURTEEN

TY, Cassidy, and Annabeth ate a late dinner together —some spaghetti with a salad and garlic bread— before playing another game of Uno.

At eight o'clock, Annabeth went to bed, giving Ty and Cassidy the chance to speak privately. Ty treasured any time the two of them had alone, especially in circumstances like these.

After Cassidy double-checked the front door, she picked up a paper from the nearby table and looked at it. "What's this?"

Ty strode closer and shrugged. "Some guy came by selling replacement windows the other day."

"Door-to-door solicitor? They usually don't come here."

"That's what I said. But I guess everyone is trying to make a living."

"Was this guy suspicious?"

Ty figured Cassidy might ask something like that. "Not really. He seemed unassuming enough."

"That's good to know at least." She deposited the brochure back on the table before hitting the lights.

Ty and Cassidy escaped to their bedroom and closed the door.

Ty listened as Cassidy updated him about everything that had happened since they'd last spoken.

Worry continued to knot in Ty's chest.

"I can't stop thinking about that phone call." Ty stood near the window, unable to sit and relax. "The one where someone said, 'We know who you are.'"

"I know." Cassidy frowned and leaned back against the headboard. "I keep thinking about that as well. I'm not sure what that's about."

"Have you felt anybody watching you?" Ty asked. "Or any inklings that you're being followed?"

Cassidy thought about his question before shaking her head. "Not really. One of the men I questioned—someone staying in a house near Seacret Escape—was watching me from his window, but that's not entirely unusual after a situation like this. I think he was just being nosy."

Ty rubbed his jaw. That might be true, but he still didn't like it.

Cassidy pulled her legs toward her chest, the picture of beautiful as the moonlight streamed through the window and illumined her blonde hair. But she wasn't just beautiful on the outside. Ty admired her on so many levels.

Cassidy cleared her throat. "We never talked about what we wanted to do."

Ty knew what she was getting at. He could hear the strain in Cassidy's voice.

In vitro fertilization.

It wasn't something that Ty ever thought he'd have to consider. But there were so many variables to contemplate about this treatment—health, time, money, the future. Some might even question the ethics of it.

"I know it's a lot of money," Cassidy said as if reading his mind.

He turned toward her, wanting to let her know he cared about every aspect of her well-being. That was his main concern. "I'm worried that it would be a lot of stress on you."

She nodded, almost sadly. "I know."

"And there's never going to be a great time for the treatments. We would have to go to Raleigh to see the doctors for this. That's going to mean taking time off work."

"I thought about that too."

He reached across the bed and grabbed her hand. "You know that every time you leave this island, it puts you at risk."

Cassidy's head hung a little lower before she raised her gaze to meet his. "There's a lot of risk. The question is, is the risk worth the reward?"

Cassidy's doctor had told her that her ovaries weren't producing enough eggs, and they'd probably not be able to get pregnant on their own.

Ty knew that more than anything Cassidy wanted a baby of her own. And he wanted to give that to her. In fact, even though the issue wasn't on his end, part of him still felt like a failure in some way.

He knew the logic didn't make sense. But that didn't stop him from feeling the way he did.

His job was supposed to be to protect her. Even though Cassidy could defend herself, Ty's instincts were to put himself between Cassidy and harm.

Yet this was a situation he couldn't fix.

Cassidy let out a long breath and played with a strand of hair. "I guess the truth is, I still don't know.

I wish I did. I wish the solutions were easy, and the answers were clear. They're not."

Ty squeezed her hand again. "We still have time."

But even as he said the words, the threat floated through his mind again.

We know who you are.

If the wrong person discovered Cassidy's true identity, then nothing would be okay. Bringing a child into a situation like that would only be foolish.

In fact, if they had a baby, then one day that very child could be in the exact same situation as Annabeth was in right now.

People with vile, hardened hearts could want to use that child to teach Cassidy a lesson. Ty also. He'd made a lot of enemies in his time as a Navy SEAL.

Ty's jaw clenched at that thought.

He wanted to fix this . . . but how?

Because there didn't seem to be a solution that would keep everyone safe.

WHEN CASSIDY ARRIVED at the office the next morning, two men wearing suits waited outside the station.

They weren't with the FBI. In fact, she'd never seen these people before.

But with their designer suits and shiny shoes, the men looked completely out of place on the island.

She paused in front of them. "Can I help you?"

The older of the two, a man who appeared to be in his late fifties, with tanned skin and white hair, took the lead. He rose and addressed her with a stiff nod. "We're here to speak with Cassidy Chambers."

"I'm Cassidy Chambers." Caution slammed into her and echoed with every heartbeat.

"Can we speak with you in private?" The man's words sounded crisp and professional.

Cassidy's curiosity grew—along with the start of suspicion. "Why don't you tell me who you are first?"

"My apologies." The man's lips flickered down in a quick frown. "My name is Will Pender, and this is Timothy Gilbert. We're attorneys with Pender, Gilbert and Associates."

"I see." Skepticism wove through Cassidy's voice. Any time she heard "attorney," her guard went up. "And where are you from?"

"Raleigh."

Raleigh? That was where the Manchesters were from as well as Governor Hollick.

A rush of anxiety shot through Cassidy, but she tamped it down.

"Follow me." She led the two into the station and turned to them as they stepped inside. "You must have either gotten here last night or you caught the very first ferry this morning, which meant you had a long night trying to get here from Raleigh."

"We arrived yesterday evening and stayed at the inn in town." Pender offered another tight nod.

"Is that right?" Cassidy took mental notes of the conversation. "Why don't we go into my office? I'd offer you some coffee, but I haven't had time to brew any yet."

"We'll be fine," Pender said.

These two guys were uptight. They hadn't cracked a smile since she met them. Cassidy's curiosity continued to grow.

She directed them to the seats across from her desk before taking her place on the other side. "Now, what can I help you with?"

Pender reached into his leather briefcase and pulled out some papers. "We're here pertaining to Annabeth Manchester."

Cassidy's breath caught, though she tried to keep her expression placid. "What about her?"

"We're lawyers for the Manchester family, and I

have signed affidavits giving permission to take the girl back to Raleigh."

Shock coursed through Cassidy. Instead of blurting the first thing that came to mind, she picked up the papers and looked at them.

All she could make out was a whole bunch of legalese and gobbledygook.

The packet looked official but that didn't mean anything.

Cassidy turned back to the two men. "Who are you representing?"

"As I said, we're lawyers for the Manchester family."

"Joe Manchester is in a coma and his wife is missing," Cassidy said. "So you're going to have to explain a little bit more than that."

No way Cassidy was letting Annabeth go with these two men. A fierce protectiveness rose up inside her at the thought of it, and she felt like a mama bear coming out of her slumber.

"I've been deemed Annabeth's guardian until her parents are able to take care of her again." Pender stared at her, carefully watching her reaction.

"And who bestowed you with that title?" Cassidy continued to press, a knot of concern forming in her gut.

She knew that neither Joe nor Alexandria had any family to speak of. The only relative that had turned up was an aunt who'd been killed in a hit-and-run on her way to Lantern Beach to pick up Annabeth.

"I'm the guardian of their estate," Pender said. "And we'd feel much more comfortable if someone associated with the Manchester family took care of Annabeth."

Cassidy leaned closer, still keeping her voice easy despite the storm raging inside. "Why did it take you so long to come here and claim her then?"

Pender swallowed. "We thought Joe and Alexandria were on vacation, and it took a while for the news to get back to us. After that, it took a few days to draw up all the proper paperwork and make sure we were taking every legal precaution necessary."

"I see." Cassidy leaned back and nodded, careful to remain in control. "But I'm afraid I can't just hand the girl over to you. There are a lot of other issues involved here."

"I understand that you'll need to talk to the social worker who's involved in this case."

"Yes, that's for starters. But I'm also going to have to talk to my own lawyer and make sure that these papers are legitimate, especially considering the circumstances around both of her parents."

"That's understood." Pender stood. "We'll be on the island for three more days, so I hope that you can resolve these matters during this time."

"We'll see about that, won't we?"

"Let us know if you have any questions." Pender gave her a nod, and then the two men left her office.

But the strange thing was, neither of the two men had asked how the girl was doing. Neither of them had asked to see her.

Somebody who was truly concerned and wanted to be Annabeth's guardian would have done one of those things, at least.

Cassidy's shoulders stiffened.

She didn't know where this was going, and she didn't like it.

CHAPTER FIFTEEN

"THESE PAPERS APPEAR to be legitimate, but, before the child is handed over to anybody, you need to go before a judge."

Attorney Ricco Salvatore stared at Cassidy from the other side of his desk. The man had been quite the legal shark back in his day, but he'd given all that up to move to Lantern Beach and set up a small private practice. He was in his sixties and wiry thin, but his actions—and his mind—were sharp.

"That's what I thought too." Cassidy paced back and forth in front of his desk. "I can't believe these guys just showed up and expected me to hand the girl over to them like this."

Ricco frowned. "The paperwork seems legal. Everything has been notarized. But there are all kinds of red flags. This isn't the standard way to do things. Why did it take them so long to show up? Who are these people?"

"That's exactly what I want to know." Cassidy's words came out faster than she intended. "And they never specified exactly who gave them legal authority over Annabeth."

"Let me look into this for you." Ricco glanced at the paperwork again. "I'll see what I can find out about these lawyers, and I'll read this paperwork word for word. Yes, sometimes that's even hard as a lawyer. These things aren't written for the common man."

"No, they're not." Cassidy had already made copies of the documents and left them in her office. She'd also called Ty to let him know what was going on. He was just as outraged as she was.

Finally, she stopped pacing and turned to Ricco. "Thank you for your help."

He straightened and squared his shoulders. "Of course. It's the least I can do for our town's police chief. I'll get back with you as soon as I know something."

With another thank you, Cassidy left the office. But she still felt wound as tight as ever.

There was so much more to this story. When

Richard Robertson had been arrested, that was just one layer of this ordeal, wasn't it? Cassidy had no idea what else hid beneath the surface.

She was about to find out.

She knew one thing: she'd fight with everything within her to protect that little girl who'd been entrusted to her care.

CASSIDY DUCKED into The Crazy Chefette to pick up a sandwich she'd ordered for lunch. She'd take it back to the office to eat so she could continue to work. With everything else going on, the situation now with Annabeth only added to the troubles pressing against her.

Plus, a storm was headed toward the island. Though forecasters weren't calling for a lot of rain, winds were supposed to be strong and the island might have some flooding. With that always came more calls for help from the community. Cassidy needed to work on this now while she could.

Just as she picked up her turkey club and turned to depart, she nearly collided with Rebecca Marks.

"I'm so sorry," Cassidy muttered. "Please excuse me. I'm a little distracted."

Rebecca waved her off. "Oh, it's no problem. I feel like I live my life in a distracted state now that I have Em."

"Sounds like a nice trade-off." Cassidy's heart twisted with a moment of envy. Em was Rebecca's toddler. Cassidy wished she knew what that was like. But she kept her expression neutral.

Only a couple of people on the island knew what she and Ty were going through. Cassidy wanted to keep the matter private.

Rebecca paused and gripped her purse. "Hey, speaking of which, any update on that case?"

"We're still working on it, but we haven't had any breaks yet. And honestly, it's no longer my investigation. The FBI rode into town and took over."

Rebecca's eyes widened. "Really? That doesn't sound good."

Cassidy shook her head. "No, it's not."

"Well, I know my two cleaners are still shaken up about what happened."

"I know . . . and then add the break-in yesterday on top of it . . ."

Rebecca's eyes widened even more. "Break-in?"

Cassidy bit the inside of her cheek. She shouldn't have brought it up, but she'd assumed that Rebecca knew. Cassidy was usually more careful than this, but lack of sleep and stress were messing with her head.

"I hope it wasn't Florence," Rebecca rushed. "She's working so hard to turn her life around."

"Turn her life around?" Cassidy shifted her weight from one foot to the other, curious about Rebecca's statement. Her turkey club was nearly forgotten.

"That's right. She's taken up a side gig to earn more money. She's really trying to get on her feet."

Cassidy's curiosity continued to spike. "Exactly what kind of side gig did she take up?"

Rebecca shrugged and waved at someone who passed before looking back at Cassidy. "I'm not sure. Florence didn't really mention any details. I figured maybe it was some type of online job or something."

Online job? Not without any internet. Florence had made a point of saying she couldn't afford it.

Cassidy stored that information away. A side gig, huh?

Maybe it was time she paid another visit to Florence. Cassidy had a few more questions for her.

CASSIDY BANGED on Florence's door and waited. A moment later, the door cracked open a couple of inches, and Florence peeked out.

"Yes, Chief?" Her voice sounded small, almost fragile.

Was the woman still shaken after what had happened? That was a possibility. The break-in had to have been traumatic.

But Cassidy suspected there was guilt behind her gaze as well.

"Can I come in?" Cassidy asked.

Florence's eyes widened. "I am afraid this isn't a good time."

"I'll only take a moment," Cassidy insisted.

"I'm sorry, Chief. But I'm in the middle of something. I . . . I can't."

Cassidy hardened her voice so the woman would know she meant business. "Florence, I can talk to you here or I can bring you down to the station to talk. It's your choice."

The woman's face seemed to go paler. Florence stared at Cassidy another moment before nodding and opening the door wider. She didn't say anything as Cassidy stepped inside.

Cassidy followed the woman to the dining room table, and they sat across from each other. A crossword puzzle book was open on the table, half of it completed. Was this what Florence had been working on? The reason she'd claimed she couldn't talk?

Florence looked up at Cassidy, questions—and a touch of fear—doing a frenzied dance in her gaze. "Can I help you with something? Did you find the person who robbed me?"

"I think you know why I'm here, Florence." Cassidy leveled her gaze with the woman, determined to get to the truth.

Florence stared back but remained silent for several seconds before finally blurting, "I don't know what you're talking about."

So she was going to do this the hard way. So be it.

Cassidy pulled some papers from her bag and spread them across the table. "I went through several files on petty crimes in this area—specifically, robberies. Mostly, they were reports from people vacationing here."

"I'm not sure what this has to do with anything . . ." Florence pushed a strand of hair behind her ear, her hand trembling.

"On each occasion, these vacationers went out as a family to the beach or to eat—leaving their house. When these families came back, they discovered something was missing from their rental. Usually, it was jewelry. Sometimes, electronics. Other times, cash."

"I heard about that. That's terrible. I can't believe how low some people sink," Florence said in a near whisper.

Cassidy's back muscles tightened as the conversation veered into even more uncomfortable territory. But she couldn't back off from this, no matter how awkward it got. "I thought maybe it was a druggie in the area trying to get money for another hit. In fact, we were never able to track down the person responsible."

"That's too bad." A touch of optimism remained in the woman's eyes.

Cassidy leaned closer, ready to make her case. "Then I cross-referenced these homes to the rental agencies they were associated with. It turns out each of the homes were ones you've cleaned before."

Florence's face went still, and her breaths became more shallow. "I've cleaned a lot of homes."

"In doing so, that means you have the keypad code to get inside most of those buildings."

"So do a lot of people in this area. Everyone at the management company can easily get their hands on those codes if they wanted to." Florence narrowed her gaze. "What are you getting at, Chief?"

Cassidy shifted, her gaze locking with Florence's. "I'm just going to ask you something point blank, Florence. Did you steal any items from the homes you've been cleaning?"

She opened her mouth, obviously about to deny it.

Before she could do that, Cassidy changed her tactic. "Actually, let me be more specific. Did you take something from the house where you found the bloody crime scene?"

The woman's hands trembled even more. "I don't know what you're talking about."

"I looked into your background, Florence. Your mom was never married. Yet you said her engagement ring was stolen."

"I . . . my mom could have had her mother's ring. An heirloom." Florence almost sounded like she was trying to convince herself as well as Cassidy. But it didn't work.

"This is what I think happened." Cassidy paused. "I think when you were in that house, you took something that didn't belong to you. Probably a ring, based on your cover story. And I think the person who killed or hurt the woman staying in that house somehow figured out you had the ring. He came back to retrieve it. Am I right?"

Florence's chin quivered.

But Cassidy said nothing. Sometimes, silence could be the best intimidation tactic.

Cassidy crossed her arms and leaned back.

She wasn't going to say a word until Florence did.

* * *

CASSIDY CONTINUED TO QUIETLY WAIT, even as the seconds slowly—painfully—ticked past.

As Florence grew more and more apprehensive,

sweat covered her fair complexion and her eyes continued to twitch.

A moment later, the woman burst into tears and buried her face in her hands.

"Yes! Yes, I did it, okay?" A sob escaped. "I don't even know *why* I did it. I just can't stand seeing these people who have all this money to burn coming here and having such a good time."

"Why is that so hard for you?" Cassidy needed to understand what Florence was thinking.

Using her sleeve, Florence wiped her eyes and looked up. "I hurt my back a few years ago. But I'm not skilled enough to do anything except clean houses. I don't have any extra money. Yet other people don't even think anything about dropping thousands on a vacation."

"So you resent them? Why don't you find a new job?"

"Like I said, I have no skills. I'd give this job up, but then I'd have no place to live and nothing to eat. Life seems so unfair."

Compassion panged inside her. But that still didn't excuse what Florence had done. "It might be unfair, but that doesn't give you the right to steal other people's belongings."

Florence swung her head back and forth, her

shoulders slumped as if she struggled to hold back a sob. "I know. You're right. The first time I stole something, I didn't sleep for a week. I kept waiting for you to knock on my door and arrest me."

"But that never happened..."

"No, so then I started to get a little braver. So I did it again. It was so easy, really. And the money .. . I thought I was going to lose this place." Florence glanced around. "Then I'd be out in the street. They already have so much. It seemed harmless .. ."

Now that Florence had admitted that, Cassidy had more questions for her. "We can talk about those other crimes a little bit later. Right now, I need to know what happened at Seacret Escape."

Florence's gaze darted back and forth as she mentally considered her options. Finally, she shrugged. "The woman who was staying there . . . I saw her when she came into the management company to check in. She was wearing the most beautiful diamond ring."

"And?"

"Later, I had to stop by and bring her some paper towels. Unlike a lot of agencies on the island, our company provides them for guests. Anyway, while I was there, the woman stepped down the hallway a moment. I noticed she'd left her ring on the table while putting on some lotion."

"So you took it?"

Florence frowned, the motion consuming her whole expression. "I knew I shouldn't take it. But I grabbed the ring and stuck it in my pocket anyway. Part of me hoped I'd get caught. Maybe if I did, I'd stop. But the woman seemed distracted and didn't even notice. I left with that ring right in my pocket."

"When was that?"

Florence frowned again. "The evening she arrived."

That would have been the day before she died if Cassidy's timeline was correct.

"Tell me about your visit with her," Cassidy prodded. "Is there anything she said that sounded suspicious? Or did she act strangely?"

Florence thought about it before letting out a long, resigned sigh. "She seemed jumpy. All the blinds were down, which I thought was weird since it was such a beautiful day outside. She wasn't wearing any beach clothes either. She was dressed in all business attire. I just couldn't figure out what she was doing on the island."

"What about anything she said? Did you have a conversation with her?"

"No," Florence said. "She thanked me for the paper towels. Then she went to get some money to tip me. We're not really supposed to take tips but . . ."

Cassidy pulled up a photo of Alexandria on her phone. "Is this the woman that you talked to?"

Florence took the phone from Cassidy and studied the picture.

And as she did, Cassidy held her breath, waiting to see what Florence would say.

CHAPTER SEVENTEEN

"I . . . I DON'T KNOW."

Disappointment filled Cassidy. "Are you sure? Look again."

Florence stared at the photo another moment before adamantly shaking her head back and forth. "It was weird because it was so dark inside the house. The woman staying at the house had tinted glasses on. Her hair was in her face. It was difficult to make out her features."

Was that on purpose? Cassidy wondered. "Do you think it could be the same person?"

Florence nodded. "It definitely *could* be the same person. The features are very similar. But I can't say for sure. I'm sorry."

Cassidy leveled her gaze with the woman. "Is

there anything else you're not telling me, Florence? It's better that you just lay it all out there now."

She remained silent for a moment before shaking her head. "No, that's it. I mean, she kind of seemed nervous. She kept looking at her phone. But I wasn't there long enough to see anything else."

"You're sure?"

Florence nodded. "I promise. I'll never steal again. Am I going to spend the rest of my life in jail?"

Cassidy pressed her lips together. This woman had admitted to stealing. Cassidy couldn't simply leave her here without any repercussions. It would be a bad example to set for the rest of the island when they found out . . . and they *would* find out. That was how small towns worked.

"I'm going to need to take you in," Cassidy said.

Florence burst into sobs again, throwing herself over the table as tears wracked her body. "I don't want to go to jail."

"Florence." Cassidy kept her voice calm. "I didn't say you were going to jail. But I *do* need to take you down to the station because we *will* press charges against you. That's how the law works, and that's what I am obligated to do."

"I have no money. People like me . . . we stay in jail for a long time."

"I have somebody I might be able to connect you with who can help," Cassidy said. "We don't have to make a big show of it. I won't even handcuff you if you promise to behave."

Florence slowly sat up as if resigned to the fact of what was about to happen. She stood and wiped the tears from her eyes. A moment later, she nodded. "Okay. Let's go."

Cassidy took her arm and led her to the police car.

At this point, Cassidy almost didn't even care about those robberies.

What she cared about was that another puzzle piece had fallen into place.

But she still had a lot more pieces to go before she got the complete picture.

CASSIDY'S THOUGHTS raced as she headed down the road—until Florence's voice cut into the silence.

"There's one other thing I just thought of," the woman said.

Cassidy glanced in the rearview mirror. "What's that?"

"The diamond ring. I don't know much about

diamonds, but I would guess it to be at least a carat. It was beautiful."

Usually, people with rings like that didn't just take them off and walk away and forget about them.

Cassidy made a mental note to check a photo of Alexandria to see what her engagement ring looked like.

"Was there anything else distinguishing about it?"

"There was one thing that I thought was interesting."

Cassidy looked in the rearview mirror again, trying to read Florence's expression. The woman kept wavering between bursting into tears and pulling herself together. The pattern seemed to repeat every five minutes.

Honestly, Cassidy felt sorry for the woman. She'd already given her a box of tissues. Now, crumpled, moist Kleenexes were scattered across her backseat.

"There was a name engraved inside the ring."

Cassidy's breath caught, and she gripped the steering wheel more firmly. "What name?"

"This is what I thought was weird. Because the name that was engraved inside was . . . Sandra."

Cassidy's heart continued to thrum in her ears.

Sandra?

The same name that the FBI agents had thrown out.

It couldn't be a coincidence.

Cassidy caught the woman's gaze in the rearview mirror. "You know, with your cooperation, we might just be able to cut you a deal, Florence."

"My cooperation?"

"Because this case is entirely bigger than you probably ever imagined."

CHAPTER EIGHTEEN

TEN MINUTES AFTER CASSIDY CALLED, Special Agent Watkins and his two wingmen showed up at the station, almost as if they had been waiting for her.

Cassidy hadn't been able to get any additional information out of them about the investigation, but they did let her listen in on their interrogation with Florence.

Unfortunately, no new information had been yielded. The good news, however, was that these guys seemed extremely interested in that ring and in the name Sandra.

There was obviously something else going on here. Cassidy just needed to figure out who this Sandra woman was.

Cassidy had already cross-referenced the name with some of the governor's family, friends, and staff. She hadn't found any matches. She'd also checked that name with the friends list on Alexandria's social media pages. But that hadn't turned up anything either.

Ricco had come to the station to act as Florence's representation. The woman would be held until her arraignment.

In the middle of everything, Ty had called and asked Cassidy to meet him at the Blackout headquarters.

Cassidy gripped the phone, trying unsuccessfully to read his tone. If he was asking this in the middle of her investigation, he had a good reason for it. "Sure, I can do that. Is everything okay?"

"It's fine. I'll explain when you get here."

Cassidy's curiosity piqued. What was so urgent that she needed to stop what she was doing to go down there? She knew Ty well enough to know he wouldn't ask unless it was important.

She left Florence in Bradshaw's care at the station before jumping in her SUV and heading down the road.

As she did, her phone rang. She glanced at the number that appeared on the screen on her dash.

She sucked in a breath.

She recognized that number.

It was the same one her threat had come from.

She hit the Talk button and got right to the point. "Who is this?"

Static crackled over the speakers, almost as if the connection was bad.

"Instructions are coming," a gravelly voice finally said.

"What kind of instructions?" Cassidy tensed as she waited for the man's answer.

"You'll see. You'll see."

As before, the line went dead.

But Cassidy's blood had gone ice cold.

She didn't want to see.

She just wanted this person to go away.

TY AND ANNABETH met Cassidy at the front door of the main building at the Blackout headquarters.

Cassidy drew on every bit of her inner strength as she plastered on a smile. She didn't want to concern Annabeth. Instead, she leaned toward the girl and ran a hand over the top of her head.

"How are you doing today, sweetie?" she murmured.

Annabeth smiled in return.

The girl had come so far even in this short amount of time. But Cassidy knew she still had a long way to go.

Cassidy looked up, and her gaze met Ty's. She was still curious as to why he'd asked her to come.

Ty took Cassidy's arm with one hand and slipped his other hand on Annabeth's back as he led them down the hallway. "The guys are going to let us use the conference room."

Conference room? What was going on here? Did this have to do with those lawyers who'd come to claim legal guardianship of Annabeth?

A bad feeling brewed in her stomach.

As they walked into the administrative area, Bethany waited there, along with her three-year-old daughter, Ada. Bethany was married to Griff, another Blackout member.

Annabeth and Ada had quickly bonded, and the two got together every chance they could.

As the two girls disappeared into another room to play with a kitchen set, Cassidy turned to Ty. She didn't bother to hide the questions in her eyes.

"What's going on?" she murmured.

"I'm sorry I couldn't share very many details. But there's someone I want you to meet. This wasn't a decision that I wanted to make on my own, so that's why I asked you to come."

Before he could explain any more, two women walked in the door. Cassidy knew one of them—Elise Locke. She was a psychologist and married to Colton, the man who headed up Blackout with Ty.

But she didn't recognize the woman beside her. The woman had bright brown eyes, a wide smile, long brown hair, and a figure so petite she almost looked like a teenager.

"Cassidy." Elise smiled warmly. "I'm glad you were able to make it. This is my friend Samantha."

"Everyone calls me Sami." The woman extended her arm and offered a surprisingly hardy handshake for such a petite woman.

"Police Chief Cassidy Chambers." Even though Cassidy trusted Elise's judgment, this meeting still made her feel cautious—especially in light of the lawyers who'd shown up today.

"Sami and I go way back," Elise continued to explain. "We were actually in college together all the way from grad school until we got our doctorates. Sami called a couple of days ago and asked if she could come visit for a while."

Sami shrugged. "I can't exactly do the very thing I tell the people I'm counseling not to do—and that would be letting my life get off-balance. I didn't take any vacations last year, and I have six weeks saved up to take this year. Why not do it here on this beautiful island with one of my best friends?"

Cassidy still wasn't sure where this was going, even though the woman seemed pleasant enough.

Elise's expression turned more serious. "Sami has an extensive background in child psychology, and she's even done some work for several police departments. I know you've been having some trouble getting the county child psychologist over here."

"I have," Cassidy said. Things were beginning to make more sense.

Elise lowered her voice. "I hope I'm not overstepping, but I talked to Sami about it, and she said she'd be more than happy to talk to you and Annabeth and see if she can offer anything to help with her recovery."

"You wouldn't mind doing that?" Cassidy turned toward Sami. "I know you said you're here on vacation."

Sami shrugged. "Honestly, I have trouble not working because I absolutely love my job. It doesn't even feel like work sometimes. That's how much I enjoy what I do."

In some ways, Cassidy understood that.

If Elise trusted this woman, Cassidy knew that she could also. Elise had proven herself to be nothing less than exemplary.

"Okay, then," Cassidy said, after getting an approving nod from Ty. "When should we set something up?"

Elise and Ty exchanged a glance.

"I can do it now." Sami shrugged, making it clear she wasn't putting pressure on anyone.

Ty turned to Cassidy. "With everything that happened today, I figured there was no time to waste."

Cassidy remembered the lawyers who'd shown up wanting to take Annabeth away. That's when she was reminded again of the urgency of the situation.

She looked at Sami and nodded. "Just let me know what you need."

CHAPTER NINETEEN

TY STOOD beside Cassidy at the back of the room as Sami sat cross-legged on the floor in front of Annabeth.

The woman was certainly friendly enough. Her eyes were warm, and she had a wide smile that put people at ease. Plus, her small size wasn't intimidating, which probably won her points with the kids she spoke with.

Annabeth didn't seem to mind the woman, even though he'd seen a spark of caution in her gaze.

Sami talked to the girl as they played with some blocks together. Some paper and crayons rested on the floor beside Sami. Maybe Annabeth could draw something that would shine more light on what had happened to her.

"I got another phone call from that same number." Cassidy said the words so quietly Ty wasn't sure he understood her.

"What?"

Cassidy continued to stare at Annabeth and Sami, her features tight and threaded with tension. "The man on the other end said I needed to wait for instructions."

"Instructions about what?" Ty had a feeling he knew that answer, but he didn't want to acknowledge it.

"Your guess is as good as mine. But I can only imagine this has something to do with his earlier statement that he knew who I was."

The tension he saw on Cassidy seemed to transfer to him. Ty's jaw tightened and his hands fisted at his side. "Someone's playing a game. And I don't like it."

Cassidy frowned. "Believe me. I don't either."

"Do you really think someone discovered your real identity?" He kept his voice low so nobody would hear.

"I can't rule out the possibility. We've always known it could happen."

Maybe they had, but . . . that didn't make this any easier.

Cassidy turned to him, her eyes wide. The vulnerability in their depths caused Ty's heart to lurch.

"I don't know what to do," Cassidy murmured.

It wasn't something Ty heard Cassidy say very often. What Ty wanted was to pull his wife into his arms and let her know that everything would be okay.

But he couldn't do that.

He didn't know that everything would be okay.

"We'll keep our eyes open," he whispered. "We'll make sure you're safe."

"Even if someone doesn't try to hurt me, what if this person *does* know my real name, and they tell the wrong people?"

Ty's jaw flexed, but he forced himself to loosen it. He didn't want to concern Cassidy even more.

"We'll cross that bridge when we get there," Ty said.

"And what about Annabeth? What if these lawyers get their way? What if they're able to take her from us?" Cassidy's voice cracked.

"Did you call Gail?" Gail was the social worker with the county who'd handled Annabeth's case.

"I did. She's having their lawyers look at things. I just have a bad feeling in my gut. I'm trying not to worry, trying to trust God that He's going to work all of this out. But, despite that, I'm still afraid."

Ty reached down and laced his fingers through Cassidy's before squeezing.

"This is a lot," he whispered. "But we're going to get through it."

Quickly, Cassidy pulled herself together and wiped beneath her eyes. She glanced at Annabeth, and Ty could see her thoughts shift.

"We can talk more later," she murmured. "Right now, I want to see what kind of progress Sami makes with Annabeth."

WHILE ADA and Annabeth went off to play, Sami approached Ty and Cassidy. She held a paper to her side.

"Annabeth is a very bright little girl," Sami said. "I was very impressed by her."

"I agree." Cassidy's gaze wandered over to where the two girls played. "I just hate that she's going through this."

"A lot of times traumatic mutism happens when someone is unable to fully process a traumatic event," Sami said. "The good news is that she doesn't seem depressed or withdrawn. If that was the case, I'd be more concerned. It would be labeled post-traumatic mutism, and then Annabeth would definitely need to be examined by a medical doctor."

"That's good news, at least." Ty crossed his arms as he waited to hear the rest of what she had to say.

"Tell me, has she spoken at all since you guys found her?" Sami asked.

Cassidy and Ty exchanged a glance.

Finally, Ty spoke. "Two weeks ago, give or take, there was a confrontation here on the island. Annabeth was supposed to stay inside, to stay away, but she snuck out. She yelled 'no' when she saw what was happening."

Sami narrowed her gaze as she listened. "What did she see?"

Ty released a long, burdened breath. "It's hard to say for certain. I don't believe she was able to see her dad. The angle was bad. But she may have seen Cassidy. Someone had a gun and was holding it on Cassidy and Annabeth's father."

Sami let out a long breath before frowning. "That's a lot."

Cassidy frowned. "I agree. It is a lot."

"I tried to see if Annabeth would repeat some words with me," Sami continued. "At first, she showed no interest. But toward the end of our time, her lips twitched, almost like she wanted to speak but was afraid to."

"Afraid . . . because of us?" Ty's voice trailed with uncertainty.

Sami quickly shook her head. "No, not because she's afraid of you. I believe that she trusts the two of you and is very comfortable with you both. Honestly, once she speaks, she probably fears she'll have to recount the whole horrible ordeal that she went through. It would be like opening a floodgate. Most likely, that's what's causing her to remain in this state. We still have a little bit more time before we become too concerned."

"What's that in your hands?" Cassidy nodded at the paper there.

"This is one reason that I believe she is comfortable with you two." Sami lifted the paper to show them. "I asked Annabeth to draw a picture of her family. As you can see with the drawing at the top, she scribbled the image of a tall man with dark hair, a woman with short dark hair, and then the girl in the dress is most likely Annabeth. I thought she was going to stop, but she kept going."

Cassidy's gaze wandered to the bottom drawing.

"Clearly, this picture at the bottom is you and

Ty." Sami pointed at the stick figures. "She's already begun to think of you like family."

Warmth spread through Cassidy's chest. It scared her how quickly she felt like she was bonding with the girl. She had to remind herself that this wasn't permanent.

She swallowed hard before asking, "Is that a good thing or a bad thing? We've gone into this knowing that it's not forever. Don't get me wrong, I'd never send Annabeth away. But I know when her father wakes up from his coma—"

"*If* he wakes up from his coma," Sami added with a pointed yet compassionate look.

"*If* he wakes up from his coma and *if* her mother is found, Annabeth will have no reason not to go back to them," Cassidy finished, trying to hold any sadness from her voice.

"It's healthy that you have that mindset." Sami glanced back at the girls. "Though attachment is good and often necessary, it can also be hard on all of the parties involved. I would like to spend more time with her in a couple of days if that's okay with you."

Cassidy and Ty glanced at each other.

"I don't see why not," Cassidy finally said.

"Great." Sami glanced at Annabeth one more

time. "She's one of those girls I just want to help. Even though she doesn't say anything, I can see her personality. I can sense the things that she's holding inside her. I just hope that you have answers for her soon."

"We all do," Ty said. "Believe me, we all do."

Just as they wrapped up the conversation, Cassidy's phone rang. It was the state crime lab. She excused herself to answer.

"Chief Cassidy Chambers." She paced to the corner for privacy.

"Chief, this is Louisa with the crime lab. I wanted to let you know we have a blood type from the samples that were brought to us from your crime scene. I know this matter is urgent, so I wanted to call you instead of simply emailing you the results."

"Okay."

"The blood type is O negative. Since you haven't discovered the victim or the victim's body, I thought this might help you narrow things down."

"It does," Cassidy said. "Thank you for calling to let me know."

As Cassidy ended the conversation, she searched her phone for a document she'd saved. A judge had authorized her to access Alexandria's medical records. That meant, Cassidy should be able to find the woman's blood type.

It took a few minutes to locate the forms she was looking for. But Cassidy finally found the information through her Cloud drive.

She held her breath as she processed what she was seeing.

Alexandria was B positive.

That meant that whoever had been involved with the crime that took place inside that beach cottage was not Alexandria.

CHAPTER TWENTY

AN HOUR LATER, Cassidy knew she had to get back to work. As much as she would like to stay at the Blackout complex with Ty and Annabeth, that wasn't an option right now considering everything that was going on.

Bethany offered to keep Annabeth with Ada so the two girls could have more playtime.

That freed up Ty to go to the station with her.

Guilt pressed on Cassidy because she knew she was taking him away from his own work. He'd sacrificed so much lately in order to take care of Annabeth, and Cassidy knew the timing wasn't great.

Ty and Colton had four new members coming to join Blackout soon. Before they arrived, Ty and Colton had a lot of preparations to make.

She was thrilled that her husband's vision for this organization was coming to life.

He deserved all the good things in this world. She wished she could give all of those good things to him. If only it were that easy . . .

Cassidy had grown up in a wealthy family where she'd wanted for nothing. She knew that having everything wasn't the recipe for happiness, no matter how it might seem sometimes. There was a lot more satisfaction found in working for the things you desired.

She and Ty walked outside. The sun shone above them, but the wind was gusty today—so much so that it was hard to speak over it. Instead, they waited until they'd climbed into Cassidy's SUV.

Before she could put it into Drive, Ty's hand covered hers. "Are you okay?"

This was finally a place they could talk without worrying about any listening ears.

But Cassidy couldn't afford to let her emotions take over right now. If she did, she might not find the strength to do everything needed back at the station.

"I just need to check in with Ricco and see if he's found out anything," she said. "These guys came from Raleigh and are staying in the area for three days. Based on how they acted, they're fully expecting to take Annabeth with them when they leave."

Ty's jaw tightened, and he glanced out the window at the fence surrounding the Blackout property. "We can't let that happen."

"I know. But if this truly is legal, it's going to be hard to stop the process. Ricco said we'll need to go before a judge. There's no way that something like this can be acted upon without that taking place."

"What do you need to do now?" Ty turned toward her. "How can I help you?"

Cassidy loved him so much for his selflessness. Before coming here, the quality was one she'd rarely encountered. So many in today's society only looked out for themselves.

"Right now, I need to go back to the office to do some more research," she finally said. "But I could always use a second set of eyes."

Ty nodded. "Of course. Whatever I can do."

Cassidy knew that he meant those words. She could always depend on Ty. Always.

CASSIDY AND TY spent the next hour at the office making phone calls and doing more research.

In the meantime, Florence had gone before the magistrate and had been released on bail. Cassidy wasn't sure where the woman had gotten the money from, but Cassidy didn't ask any questions and let Ricco handle it instead.

Every time she let her thoughts wander, they always went back to her phone call.

Instructions are coming.

Cassidy could practically feel a train headed toward her, yet she was unable to get off the tracks. She didn't know what to do to stop the inevitable.

Nausea roiled in her stomach at the thought of it.

Dear Lord, You're in control. Please help me now.

As someone knocked at her door, Cassidy looked up, fully expecting to see either one of her officers or Paige standing there.

Instead, it was another familiar face.

Cassidy rose from her desk, her pulse quickening. "Governor Hollick?"

What in the world was he doing here?

CHAPTER TWENTY-ONE

"MAY I HAVE A WORD WITH YOU?" Hollick asked Cassidy before glancing at Ty. "In private?"

Cassidy pressed her palms into her desk as she addressed the governor. "Anything that you need to say to me, you can say in front of my husband."

Hollick hesitated a moment, as if unsure about her statement. The man looked like he'd aged since the last time Cassidy had seen him. He was in his fifties, with thinning brown hair and a lean build. The man favored wearing khakis and white button-up shirts, but the look only added to his uptight disposition.

Finally, he nodded and took a seat beside Ty. "Very well then."

"Are you here alone?" As Cassidy lowered herself

back into her seat, she tried to put the pieces together. Last time Hollick had been here, he had a team of four security officers with him. Roads had to be cleared. Officials had to be notified.

"I am here alone." Hollick offered a tight nod of affirmation.

Cassidy twisted her neck just enough to show her curiosity. "Why would you leave your protection detail behind?"

"It's a long story." Hollick shifted and frowned. "And it's really not important."

If the man had gone through all that trouble to get away without his security team, then it *did* seem important. But Cassidy kept her mouth closed and waited for whatever else he had to say.

"I'm only here because the matter is urgent," he continued.

Urgent? Last time he was here, the matter had been urgent, to say the least.

Richard Robertson had tried to force the governor's doctor to inject Hollick with a medication that would mimic the symptoms of ALS, as a matter of revenge. Thankfully, Cassidy and her crew had stopped him before that happened. The whole event had been dramatically Hollywood-worthy.

Did Hollick's presence here have something to do with Robertson?

The governor leveled his gaze with Cassidy. "It's like this. I know who you really are, Cassidy."

CASSIDY FELT the blood drain from her face.

Certainly, she hadn't heard Governor Hollick correctly.

He couldn't possibly be talking about . . .

"You know who I really am?" she repeated.

But even as the words left Cassidy's lips, she felt the tension crackling across the room. If this was the truth . . . then her life had just made a pivot that would be hard to recover from.

Hollick frowned, the lines on his face deepening. "That's right. Now, I don't know what to do about it."

Cassidy had to think quickly here. Her life—and future—depended on her response. She couldn't admit anything—not unless she absolutely had to. The man could be bluffing. Or she could have misunderstood.

Cassidy forced herself to look unflustered on the outside—even if her insides felt like a ball of stress.

"I'm afraid I don't know what you're talking about, Governor."

Hollick leaned forward, his elbows perched on his legs as he stared her in the eye. "I have the news articles . . . Cady Matthews."

When Cassidy heard him say her name, everything went still around her. Hollick wasn't joking. He really *did* know about her past. There'd been no misunderstandings.

Cassidy swallowed hard, knowing she still needed to play this safe. "Who is Cady Matthews?"

An unreadable emotion flickered in Hollick's gaze. "You don't have to play dumb. I've seen the proof, and I know that you two are the same person."

Cassidy wasn't ready to admit anything. Not yet. Instead, she decided to shift the focus of the conversation. "I don't understand why you came here to say these things."

Exactly what was Hollick's endgame right now? Even if he'd discovered this information, *how* had he discovered it? Why had he gone looking? And why was he bringing it to her now?

The governor's shoulders seemed to slump. "I'm coming here with this information because I need your help."

Her help? Would this be a bad time to mention

that Cassidy felt less inclined to help people who were holding something over her head? She had no choice but to listen to him—not just because of his position, but because she had to know more.

Her gaze flickered to Ty. He seemed equally as riveted—and off-balance—by the conversation. But he remained quiet, letting Cassidy navigate this.

Her gaze went back to Hollick. She observed the way the man's leg fidgeted. The sweat on his upper lip. His unsteady gaze.

He was nervous also.

She stored away that fact.

"What do you mean when you say you need my help?" Cassidy finally asked.

Everything seemed to fade around her—everything except Ty—as she waited for Hollick's response. Cassidy couldn't stop thinking about her husband. About how things could change between them in the blink of an eye if she weren't careful. Or if she didn't handle the situation correctly. Or if she owned up to too much. Or if she didn't own up to enough.

Her future seemed to teeter on this moment.

Hollick leaned closer and lowered his voice. "I'm going to tell you something, but I need your discretion."

"You do know that I am an officer of the law."

His eyes narrowed. "And you do realize that I have influence here in the state. I'd hate for someone in the county to find out there was a police chief in the area who's using an alias instead of her real name."

Cassidy sucked in a quick breath. The man had a point.

She wasn't sure what he was about to say. But it looked like they both had things at stake here. Moral obligations. Choices. Maybe even regrets.

"Understood," Cassidy finally said. "You have my discretion."

Hollick nodded slowly, almost somberly. Whatever he had to say, the words weighed on him and practically aged him, for that matter.

"Last night, I got an email," he finally said. "And that's when this all started."

CHAPTER TWENTY-TWO

TY FELT the tension spread across his shoulders as he sat in the seat beside Hollick, waiting for the man to continue.

It was one of those moments like he'd experienced in the Middle East—the moments where his life was on the line and one wrong move would put him in the enemy's hands.

When one wrong move would mean the choice between life and death.

A pendulum moment. That was what Ty had called them.

Ty and Cassidy had spoken of times like that since then. They'd both agreed they existed.

And that they were terrible.

It was agonizing to know that one event—one

five-minute interlude—could change the entire course of a life.

He glanced at Cassidy. Her face was tight. Her motions were jerky. Her eyes almost seemed unsteady.

To him, at least.

Most people looking at her would think she was calm and in control. But Ty knew her well enough to know better.

This whole conversation had shaken her to the core . . . and it wasn't over yet.

Ty had a feeling this could get worse before it got better.

Cassidy remained cool as she asked, "What kind of email did you get last night?"

"The email contained two different voice recordings," Hollick said.

"What were these recordings about?"

Ty sensed the governor hesitating. The man didn't want to talk about this. But Hollick must be desperate if he'd come all the way to Lantern Beach to speak with Cassidy.

Hollick licked his lips, a certain sense of defeat capturing him. "The audio was recorded in secret. Listening to it, it sounds like I'm making a deal with my brother to give funding for that ALS medication to him instead of to Buxton Pharmaceuticals. But it was a casual conversation—that's all."

Ty sucked in a quick breath. He wasn't so sure about that. But he'd give the governor the benefit of the doubt . . . for now.

"Are you sure that's not what you did?" Cassidy asked point-blank.

Atta girl. Ty had always loved the fact that Cassidy spoke her mind. Even more so, she knew when to speak her mind and when to keep quiet. Strategy was everything in these situations.

"The conversations we had were real." Hollick tugged at his pant leg, clearly uncomfortable. "But they were taken out of context. When you listen to the recordings, it sounds like I'm making a deal for my own benefit. But that's not what happened."

Ty had a lot of doubts about that, but he kept his mouth closed—for now.

Cassidy's jaw visibly tightened as she slowly nodded. "We'll get back to those conversations in a minute. How did someone even get their hands on those recordings?"

Hollick shifted again, the sweat on his upper lip thickening. "My brother and I had these conversations in the privacy of my home. Looking back, they were a bad idea. But the recordings cut off right before the point in our talk where I refused."

Cassidy narrowed her eyes. "So someone bugged your home? Who would have done that?"

Hollick frowned. "Without exposing the recordings to more people, it's hard to know. But my first guess would be Robertson. He's the only one that makes sense."

Ty shook his head, unable to remain quiet. "If Robertson had evidence like this, he would have gone public with it. He wouldn't have tried to teach you a lesson himself when he could have just released that audio and ruined your life that way, don't you think?"

Hollick shifted again, crossing and uncrossing his legs. The conversation clearly made him uncomfortable. "I know. I thought about that. And I do wonder if he was going to play this as a wild card after his original plan had been implemented."

"That still doesn't explain how someone got their hands on those recordings and sent them to you via email," Cassidy said. "Robertson is in jail. It couldn't have been him."

"I know. Unless he saved the files on the computer or gave them to somebody."

"In other words . . . if he was working with someone," Cassidy muttered before pressing her lips together as if disturbed.

Hollick went paler. "Exactly."

Cassidy narrowed her gaze and leaned closer. "But why are you here now? Why come to me with this information? And why did someone tell you that I'm secretly someone else."

Ty stiffened as he listened closely, anxious to hear where this conversation would go.

Nowhere good, he was certain of that.

"These people also sent me instructions," Hollick said. "They said if I didn't expose you for who you really are then the person who sent me the audio files was going to make them public. He gave me three days."

Ty sucked in a breath. Hollick was being blackmailed. But why did someone want to expose Cassidy that badly? How could that revelation possibly benefit someone? And why didn't they leak the information themselves?

DH-7, the gang who'd originally put out a hit for Cassidy, didn't operate this way. This method was too sophisticated for them.

Ty's mind raced as he tried to find answers.

Cassidy leaned back again, her gaze focusing as if she was formulating her next step. "Let me get this straight. Someone has incriminating evidence on you. But for some reason, they want *you* to expose *me*? Why would someone go after a small-town police chief when they could take down a governor?"

Hollick frowned. "That's what I'm wondering also."

Cassidy's eyes traveled back and forth, back and forth, back and forth.

Finally, she asked, "So what are you going to do?"

Ty's gaze went to the governor as he waited for his response.

CASSIDY'S HEART pounded in her ears as she waited to hear Hollick's answer.

Her future rode on his choice.

Hollick released a long breath. "I don't know what to do. That's why I came here. You saved my life, Cassidy. I can be selfish, power-hungry, and a myriad of other less-than-flattering adjectives. But the one thing I'm not is stupid."

Cassidy couldn't be too quick to believe him—and definitely not too quick to trust the man. "Tell me, do you have any idea who might have sent them? Is there anybody besides Robertson?"

Hollick tugged at his pant leg again. "I have all kinds of enemies. But the only people who make sense are people who are connected with Robertson."

Cassidy nodded slowly, letting that sink in. She supposed Robertson could have hired other people to carry on with his dirty work, even if he died.

Hollick rubbed the edge of Cassidy's aging desk where several small chips were missing from the wood. He seemed to need the distraction to compose himself. "I was hoping you might have some answers for me."

How much could Cassidy tell him? She thought about it a moment before making up her mind. "Let's just say that the mystery surrounding Alexandria Manchester isn't over yet."

Cassidy gave him a brief update on what had transpired over the past week.

Hollick seemed to grow paler and his eyes more haunted with every new detail. "So you're telling me that the people holding Alexandria captive are still out there and still working on some type of angle that we're not clear about?"

Cassidy offered a curt nod. "Yes, that's exactly what I'm saying. And while we're talking about it, does the name Sandra ring any bells?"

The governor thought about it a moment before shaking his head. "I can't say it does. Why?"

"The name has come up in the investigation, but we haven't been able to identify anyone. I should also let you know that the FBI are now involved."

A flash of surprise registered in his eyes. "The FBI?"

There was only one natural connection Cassidy could come up with. "Do you think they suspect that you're involved in this somehow?" That would explain the national security comment Watkins had made . . . maybe.

"I can assure you that I am *not* involved with that little girl's abduction. White-collar crimes? Maybe. But something like an abduction or kidnapping? Never."

Had the governor just admitted he was involved in crimes? Cassidy would address that later. "How long are you staying in town, Governor Hollick?"

"I'm heading back after this conversation. I can't afford for people to ask too many questions. I told everyone I was going for a drive to clear my head and to not expect me back for the rest of the day."

"And you don't know what you're going to do?" Ty asked.

His gaze darkened. "The feds are already investigating me. If people find these audio files, my career will be dead. Not only that, but I could spend time in jail. I can't let that happen."

Cassidy read between the lines. Hollick wouldn't sacrifice himself to save Cassidy. It didn't matter what she'd done for him, even if that meant she'd risked her own life for his.

His response didn't surprise her.

But this wasn't a done deal yet.

"I need you to do me a favor," Cassidy said. "I need you to give me some time to figure this out before you do anything."

"How much time are you talking?"

"The person threatening you gave you three days?"

"That's right."

"Then give me two. Is it a deal?"

The governor stared at her, and, as Cassidy waited for his answer, she realized how much she hated putting her future in this man's hands.

CHAPTER TWENTY-THREE

AS SOON AS Governor Hollick left, Ty rose from his seat, crossed the room, and pulled Cassidy into his arms. She didn't resist the embrace. In fact, she buried herself in her husband's arms.

"The noose is tightening," Cassidy murmured into Ty's chest. "The governor knows who I am. Someone told him. That means there are people out there who know my true identity. If word leaks . . ."

"Don't talk like that."

"It's hard not to, especially with so much on the line." Cassidy pulled away just enough to glance up at Ty. "What if my identity is leaked? I won't be able to stay here on Lantern Beach. And you have Hope House and Blackout and—"

He gently shushed her. "We'll figure all that out. Wherever you are, that's where I'm going to be also."

"But you shouldn't have to live in hiding—"

"Cassidy." Ty locked his gaze with hers, clearly trying to stop her panic before it spun out of control. "We're going to figure this out."

She stepped back and squeezed the skin between her eyes. She wished she believed those words. But right now, all she felt was panic. She couldn't remember the last time she'd felt this edgy.

"I don't know how," she murmured. "I can't believe someone found out this information. We covered our tracks. This wasn't supposed to happen."

"Somebody found out the information about the governor also. We need to ask ourselves how this person is doing this."

"There's only one way that I can think of." Cassidy paused and straightened her shoulders. "Whoever is behind this has to be able to get into our computer systems somehow. It's the only thing that makes sense."

A knot formed between Ty's eyebrows. "You mean, like a hacker?"

"Yes, I mean like a hacker. If someone put bugs in the governor's place somehow, then we need to check everything to make sure we haven't been bugged also."

"I can have my guys help us with that."

Cassidy began pacing in her small office. "I don't even know if I can trust Hollick."

Ty's hands went to his hips as he stood near the wall watching Cassidy. "It would be wise not to. The man has a lot on the line also. Desperate people will take desperate measures."

She snapped her gaze back up to meet his. "I have two days to figure this out, Ty. How am I going to do that?"

"We'll figure it out. Somehow. I'll keep checking and digging, and we'll find answers. Maybe we should start with that name. Sandra."

It was a logical place to start but . . . "I've searched everything I can think of trying to find a connection with that name. I haven't had any luck."

"Then maybe you should have a heart-to-heart conversation with the FBI."

Cassidy's startled gaze met his. "And tell them who I am?"

"No, not that." Ty swung his head back and forth, leaving no doubt where he stood on that issue. "But we need to get more information from them about why they're here. Once we know that, maybe we'll finally have some of those answers you've been looking for."

Cassidy remained still, contemplating his words before nodding. "You're right. But now I have to think of a way to either convince them to share or, if that doesn't work, think of a less-than-savory way to find out."

Ty was right. Desperate people did desperate things.

And, right now, Cassidy was the desperate one.

AFTER A FEW MORE MINUTES OF thought, Cassidy offered Ty a resolute nod. "I'm going to give Agent Watkins a call. It can't hurt to ask, right?"

Ty nodded. "It sounds like a plan to me."

Drawing in a deep breath, Cassidy picked up her phone and dialed the agent's number. He answered on the second ring.

"Special Agent Watkins, this is Chief Chambers." Cassidy lowered herself into the chair behind her desk. "I was hoping the two of us might meet."

"Funny that you said that." His voice sounded dry and humorless.

Cassidy narrowed her eyes. "Why's that?"

"I just got a call from Governor Hollick. He requested that I let you help out on this case as a personal favor."

Cassidy drew in a breath. She hadn't been expecting that. But she was thankful the governor had put in a good word for her.

"So what do you think?" Cassidy knew she had to use every angle possible.

Watkins hesitated a moment before answering. "I can be at your station in ten minutes. But you're not a part of this investigation."

"I understand." At least he was meeting with her. It was a good start.

Right now, Cassidy just had to concentrate on finding answers. She'd worry about everything else later.

As she ended the call, she turned to Ty and gave him the update.

"The governor actually pulled through, huh?" Surprise washed through Ty's gaze. "I wish I could say I wasn't surprised, but I am."

"Me too. I'm still on the fence about how I feel about the man."

"It would be wise to keep Hollick at arm's length. He only thinks about one person—himself."

"I know." Cassidy wasn't naïve. Part of her work

involved knowing when to and when not to trust people. Choosing unwisely could mean life or death. "I know the only reason Hollick put in a good word was to help his own cause. But maybe I can use his desperation to help us as well."

"Let's hope."

Cassidy needed to get her thoughts together and prepare herself for the conversation with Watkins. As she glanced at Ty, she realized he couldn't be here for the meeting.

He seemed to read her mind.

"I'm going to call a friend to give me a ride back to Blackout so I can pick up Annabeth and my truck. If you need me, call."

"I will." Cassidy stood and kissed Ty's cheek.

Now she had to get ready for her talk with Watkins.

She hoped it was fruitful . . . because so much depended on it.

CHAPTER TWENTY-FOUR

RIGHT ON TIME, Watkins arrived. As usual, he looked stiff and formal as he sat across from Cassidy in her office.

"I'm not obligated to tell you anything." An edge of defensiveness crept into his voice.

Cassidy had figured he might respond like that. "I realize that. But this is also my island, and it's my job to keep the people here safe. Any cooperation we could have with each other in this case would be appreciated. Plus, maybe there's some way I can help without getting involved."

He grunted but remained otherwise silent. Finally, he wiped his hands on his dress slacks, straightening the legs as he readjusted his seating position.

"Three days before your crime scene was discovered, one of our agents who works out of the Raleigh Field Office suddenly disappeared," Watkins finally said, a sigh-like quality to his words. "Her name was Sandra Myers."

That explained the name, at least.

"What do you mean when you say 'disappeared'?" Cassidy was curious about the details.

"She didn't come into work that morning. She called in sick, but Sandra was never sick, nor had she indicated the night before that she was getting sick. It was very unlike her."

"It's not a crime to take a day off, right?"

"No, it's not," Watkins said. "But she'd been acting suspiciously lately, and my boss asked me to keep an eye on her. We pinged her phone. It led to the island."

Cassidy tried not to show the thrill she felt at the fact she was actually making progress. This was the information she'd been looking for. "So Sandra was here on Lantern Beach?"

"She was staying in that house where the blood was discovered."

Cassidy drew in a quick breath upon hearing the confirmation. "So you think that whatever she was involved with got her hurt?"

Watkins offered a tight nod. "That's the theory we're working on. So far, we have no leads. We've followed several different theories, but we haven't had any success in finding concrete answers."

"I'm sorry to hear that. Do you plan on staying here on the island until she's found?"

"That hasn't been decided yet." Watkins rolled one of his meaty shoulders back as if trying to loosen up. "But we would like some conclusion before we leave."

"Understood." At least, Cassidy had a better idea what was going on.

Watson focused his laser-like eyes on Cassidy. "Is there anything of note *you'd* like to share?"

Several thoughts raced through Cassidy's mind. Annabeth. The threat against the girl. The information the governor had shared.

But none of those things seemed relevant to what the feds were looking into.

But Cassidy knew she should offer something to build rapport. "I found out earlier that the blood type from the crime scene, O negative, didn't match the victim who was supposedly staying in the house. I wondered who'd really been staying there. May I see a picture of Sandra Myers?"

A moment later, Watkins showed her a photo on his phone.

Cassidy's eyes widened. The woman who stared back looked eerily similar to Alexandria Manchester, from the brown hair all the way down to her build.

Had someone planned it that way? Was this all a ruse? And if so, why?

Watkins narrowed his gaze at her. "You look like you're thinking about something."

"Special Agent Myers looks a lot like the woman whose name was on the rental agreement for that house. But I'm sure you know that."

He nodded. "We've looked into this Alexandria Manchester woman. We believe that, for some reason, Special Agent Myers was able to obtain Mrs. Manchester's driver's license and that she registered to rent the house under a fake identity. Why did she choose Mrs. Manchester's name? We're not sure. We don't believe there are any notable links between those two women."

Cassidy repressed a shiver. She didn't know what was going on here, but it just kept getting stranger and stranger.

Watkins shifted, as if ready to depart as soon as

he could. "Is there anything else that could be helpful?"

Cassidy shook her head, knowing she'd told him everything relevant. "I told you what I know."

Too much was on the line, and Cassidy needed more answers. Her next moves could mean life or death so she had to choose wisely.

Watkins extended his arm, and the two exchanged a handshake.

"If you discover anything, I'd appreciate hearing about it," Watkins said.

"Of course. And I'd love that same courtesy in return."

Watkins looked away, not promising that he would help. But he hadn't given her an outright no either.

Before Watkins stepped away, Paige appeared at the door.

"You're both probably going to want to know this." Paige's expression looked pinched. "Fred Idles just called. The storm that's churning offshore drew several feet of water out of the Pamlico Sound. When it did, Fred found . . . a body located about twenty-five yards or so from his place."

"A body?" Cassidy repeated.

"That's right. He sounded really upset."

Cassidy exchanged a look with Watkins.

Cassidy knew how she'd be spending the rest of her day.

The question was whose body was it?

Alexandria's?

Sandra's?

Or someone entirely different?

CASSIDY PULLED UP TO FRED IDLES' place with Special Agent Watkins. Fred's bungalow was located at the end of a long gravel lane, not far from the cottage Cassidy had investigated with Bradshaw, Ranger, and Dillinger.

Though Fred's house was small, the structure was raised up on stilts and had been painted a cheerful turquoise color.

The island native was a fixture and someone Cassidy often talked to at church. He liked to share seafood recipes and tell stories about storms he'd lived through here on the island.

As Cassidy and Watkins stepped out of her SUV, the wind brushed across them, tugging Cassidy's hair from her bun. Watkins' fellow agents were on their way, as were two of Cassidy's officers.

"I've never seen anything like this," Agent Watkins muttered as he stared out at the Pamlico Sound.

The front that was coming had pulled the water at least a half a mile out. Cassidy had seen the phenomenon a couple of times since she'd lived here on the island. All that remained where the water had once been was the wet sediment normally found on the seabed. The mucky sand was dotted with seagrass and clams and the occasional crab pot or broken cement brick—usually used to anchor small watercraft.

Cassidy motioned for Watkins to follow her as she started toward the house in the distance. "We don't have much time."

"What do you mean?"

"I mean, it only took about an hour for this water to go out. It will take less time for it to come back."

"Really?" Watkins almost sounded alarmed.

"This isn't even a huge system," Cassidy explained. "When hurricanes come through and cause a negative storm surge like this one, the water can rush back like a tidal wave. The Pamlico can stretch from one side of the island all the way to the ocean."

"It doesn't sound . . . safe."

"That's life living on a barrier island."

Cassidy hid her smile. She liked seeing Watkins look a little off-balance.

They reached Fred, who stood at the base of the steps leading to his house. The man was in his seventies, and he walked with a hunched back and slow steps. But he never let that stop him from getting around.

"Hi, Fred. This is Special Agent Watkins with the FBI. He'll be assisting me today." Cassidy hid another smile when the agent grunted. "We heard you discovered something we should see."

"When the water went out, I decided to go grab some clams. This is the best time to get them—they're just out there for anyone to see. The birds love them. Just look."

Cassidy followed the line of his finger and spotted several seagulls diving at the wet sand.

"I just didn't expect to see what I saw." Fred's face looked pale.

Cassidy squeezed his arm, sensing the trauma he was facing. "It's okay. Can you show us where you found the body?"

He stretched his arm out again and pointed to something in the distance. "It's right there. Can't miss it. Do I need to go with you?"

"I think we can manage. Why don't you just sit down and get yourself something to drink?" The last thing Cassidy wanted was for the man to have a medical emergency because of the stress of the situation.

Fred nodded. "I can do that."

Watkins narrowed his gaze as he turned to Fred. "You didn't touch anything, did you?"

"No. Honestly, I thought it was an old trash bag or something someone had left out there. When I saw what it actually was . . . I definitely didn't want to touch anything."

"You did great. Thank you." Cassidy nodded again before heading toward the sand.

Watkins' tone irritated her. There was no need to talk to Fred as if he was somehow involved in this. Fred was an exemplary citizen.

Cassidy glanced at Watkins as they started across the receded waterline. "I hope you don't like your shoes."

"My shoes?" He glanced down.

"The sand is mucky. It will feel like you're being suctioned to the bottom." She glanced at his glossy loafers. "I'm sure it'll wash out."

He looked at her again before taking his first step into the water-logged sand. As soon as his shoe began to sink into the sediment there, he quickly stepped back. He took his shoes and socks off, then rolled up the legs of his dress slacks.

As he did, Cassidy continued toward the body. She'd meant it when she said they didn't have much time. That water could be back at any minute. It was anyone's guess how quickly the Pamlico would come back or how deep it would be when it did.

The rest of the crew was due to arrive anytime to help retrieve the body. But first, Cassidy and Watkins needed to document as much about the body as possible.

Cassidy heard sloppy steps behind her and saw Agent Watkins hurrying toward her through the wet sand.

Again, she hid a smile. He was a fish out of water in this area, and it was nice to see him a little humbled.

"It smells like . . . fish around here," he muttered as he caught up.

"That's the scent of the sea." Cassidy didn't know what else to say to that remark. At first, it had bothered her. But now, the scent reminded her of home.

Her smile dropped.

Home.

Cassidy hoped she was able to keep calling this place home. But ...

She'd think about that later.

Finally, they stopped beside the body. Any of Cassidy's remaining humor disappeared as she stared down at the corpse—a corpse now decomposing with the help of fish, crabs, and the sea.

CHAPTER TWENTY-FIVE

WATKINS KNELT beside the body and used a pen from his pocket to lift strands of wet hair from the woman's face.

Cassidy could only look at the woman for a few seconds before averting her gaze to Watkins.

The agent closed his eyes, almost as if in reverence.

"It's Sandra." His voice cracked.

"I'm so sorry." Cassidy truly was. The man had obviously considered the woman a friend. In the least, she'd been a colleague.

His jaw flexed as he opened his eyes and looked in the distance. His gaze then traveled back, and Watkins studied Sandra's remains a moment, a new determination in his gaze.

"It looks like someone chained cement blocks to her foot and arm to keep her body from floating up." His voice sounded terse.

"The water here is probably only three feet deep, at the most, on ordinary days," Cassidy told him. "Whoever dumped Sandra's body here probably thought they went out far enough to make sure she would remain underwater. They probably figured the elements would take care of her before anyone found her."

"So it probably wasn't someone local behind this," Watkins muttered. "Or they would've known the water would recede with the approaching storm."

"I agree."

Cassidy looked at the waterline in the distance, wondering if the Pamlico was getting closer or farther away. She couldn't afford to *not* think about it.

She turned back to Watkins. "I'm going to have to guess, based on the amount of blood I saw at the scene, that this woman died there, and someone disposed of her body here."

"I think you're right. I *hope* you are. No one should die this way."

Cassidy glanced at Sandra's body again,

searching for any signs as to what had happened. But the water had washed away most of the evidence. At least now Watkins and his guys could have some closure. It was better than living with haunting questions and unknowns.

Cassidy stared at the horizon again. This time, she sucked in a breath.

"What's wrong?" Watkins glanced up at her.

"The water . . . it's coming back. Fast."

He followed her gaze, and his eyes widened. "How much time do we have?"

"Not enough. We need to take a few pictures. Then we need to get Sandra's body to the shore. Otherwise, any remaining evidence could be destroyed."

Without another word, the two of them got busy.

CASSIDY'S BACKUP, along with the other two FBI agents, arrived just in time with a body bag. Everyone worked quickly to secure Sandra's body—including the cement blocks that had been tied to her arm and leg.

After they moved the body, Cassidy and Watkins took a few more photos with their phones of the sediment around the body just in case any clues had been left there. Cassidy collected as many samples as she could, just in case.

When Cassidy looked back, the water was probably only thirty feet away.

Without wasting more time, Cassidy and Watkins raced back to the shore.

She heard the water rushing behind her, coming in quickly and right at their heels.

Watkins hurried along beside her, looking over his shoulder every few seconds.

Finally, they reached Fred's house and began climbing the stairs just as the water rushed beneath them.

The rest of the crew had already scrambled onto the second story deck with Sandra's body.

Cassidy and Agent Watkins continued to ascend the steps. Just as they reached the top, the water completely surrounded the house.

Thankfully, they'd parked farther up the lane, where the land was higher.

Cassidy held her breath as she waited to see how elevated the water would be.

Would it reach her vehicle? Total it? Strand them here for a while?

Instead, the waves lapped at the property's edge.

But it didn't go any further.

That was something else to be thankful for.

Now they needed to send Sandra for an autopsy. Though Doc Clemson was the coroner on the island, Cassidy had a feeling the FBI would want to use someone of their own choosing for this—most likely someone with the state. She couldn't blame them. This victim had been one of their own, and she would do the same in their shoes.

Watkins shook his head and let out a little chuckle as he stared down at the Pamlico Sound. "In all my years, I've never experienced anything like that before. This island ... it sure is different."

Cassidy turned her face away from the breeze. "There's a reason why the people who've lived here for generations are so tough. They've been through a lot. They've had to show courage and always be ready for a little adventure. That's probably why I love the area so much."

Before they could talk any more, Cassidy's phone buzzed.

She glanced at the screen and saw she had a new text message.

Her eyes widened when she read the words there.

. . .

THAT COULD BE YOU.

HER BACK MUSCLES PINCHED.

She glanced around, searching for anyone nearby who might be watching.

She only saw trees, marsh grass, and the Pamlico Sound.

But someone had obviously been aware of what they were doing.

And this person was making a very clear threat.

CHAPTER TWENTY-SIX

CASSIDY FELT WATKINS' studious eyes on her.

"Is everything okay?" An edge of suspicion lined his voice.

She quickly put her phone back into her pocket, careful to conceal any concern she felt. "Everything's fine. Just a follow-up text about another case."

He stared at her a moment before nodding and looking back at the ground below. "What now? Will the water recede?"

"Eventually. In the meantime, we need to talk about your friend's body."

"I'll handle it." His jaw hardened again, the way it did when a subject wasn't open for discussion.

"That's what I thought. If you find out anything

of note, I'd appreciate the courtesy of being kept in the loop."

"If I can, I will. But killing a federal investigator is a felony punishable by the death penalty. Whatever's happening here . . . it just got bigger. The Bureau will put even more men and women on this now."

"I can't blame them for that." Another question lingered in Cassidy's mind, one that only this agent could help her with. There was no better time than now to ask—now while they were stuck here on this deck together. "Agent Watkins, can I ask you a question? In private?"

His jaw tensed again as if he was uncomfortable at the mere idea of what she might ask. Finally, he nodded and walked with her away from any listening ears.

He crossed his arms as he turned toward her. "What can I help you with?"

"Do you know anything about a couple by the names of Lars and Emma Shackleford?"

A moment of recognition flashed in his gaze. But his expression remained guarded and hesitant. "What about them?"

"I understand that they used to work for the US government. For the CIA, for that matter."

"I'm familiar with who they are, and that's

correct. They were with the CIA. But the two of them left on bad terms. They were fired."

"They were accused of selling information to Russia, is that right?"

"Correct. They knew they were about to be arrested, and that's when they ran."

Cassidy nodded, trying to keep her expression neutral. "I suppose that the evidence against them was pretty convincing."

"You could say that. I'd call it irrefutable. They were both facing life in prison. The assistant director, Gerald Mecklenburg, found the evidence himself."

"And since then they've been on the run?" Cassidy's heart thrummed with eagerness as she waited for his response.

"Yes. They've been stirring up trouble. I guess it only proves the Shacklefords were never on the side of what was right. They're wanted for at least eight murders now, among other things."

Cassidy repressed a shiver at his reminder. "So you'd say that these guys are dangerous."

"Absolutely. Why?" Watkins narrowed his eyes as he waited for her answer.

"They were involved with the case concerning North Carolina Governor Hollick. We believe a man by the name of Richard Robertson hired them. We also believe they still might be holding Manchester's wife, Alexandria, captive. By default, it seems as if they could be involved with this case also."

Watkins' expression tightened. "I'm not sure what the two of them killing Sandra would prove."

Cassidy crossed her arms. "I'm not sure either. But maybe that's what we need to figure out."

THE WATER RECEDED AS QUICKLY as it came in, enough for Cassidy and the rest of the gang to get back to their vehicles.

With that situation now being out of her jurisdiction, Cassidy climbed into her SUV and went to visit Ricco again. She needed to know if there were any updates on Annabeth and the lawyers trying to claim guardianship of the girl.

As Cassidy glanced down at her uniform, she frowned. She wished she'd taken some time to go back and change. Muddy sand covered her shoes, and the edges of her pant legs were still wet. She could only imagine how her hair looked. No doubt, loose strands had spread out from her bun.

But, right now, there were too many other things to worry about.

"Chief." Ricco paused from where he sorted files on his desk. "I was hoping that you'd stop by."

Cassidy didn't bother to sit down. She was too wired. "Have you found out anything?"

He put his folders on his desk and gave her his full attention. "As a matter of fact, I did. I spoke with a judge, and he's put a halt on these orders while he reviews the circumstances."

Cassidy released her breath. "That's a relief."

"Yes, it is. This isn't over. But I don't see how this paperwork is going to hold up in a court of law. I found some questionable wording in the depths of the document."

"Let's hope it doesn't, especially considering everything that's going on and how much danger Annabeth has been in since all of this started."

"I agree." Ricco tilted his head as he addressed Cassidy. "There's something else that I thought you might want to know."

Tension threaded across her chest as Cassidy anticipated what he might have to say. "What's up?"

"I have some lawyer friends in Raleigh, so I've made a few calls to look into the attorneys who filed the paperwork to gain custody of Annabeth."

"And?" Cassidy nearly held her breath as she waited to hear what he had found out.

"I had to do a little bit of digging, but it turns out that Clark Pender himself is currently under investigation with the state disciplinary board."

Her breath caught. "For what?"

"He supposedly broke a confidentiality agreement and blabbed some details about a case he was handling. He got drunk and then chatty with a woman he met at a bar. The problem was this woman actually knew the prosecutor for the case and told him what had happened. Talk about a stroke of bad luck." Ricco clucked his tongue and shook his head.

"Do you think that fact has something to do with all of this?"

Ricco shrugged, obviously hesitating to say anything definitive—just like any good lawyer might. "I'm not saying it does. I'm not saying it doesn't either. I just thought I'd mention it to you, just in case."

All the pieces swirled in Cassidy's mind.

Somebody was holding incriminating audio recordings over the governor. Holding the truth about her past over Cassidy. They'd possibly been holding something over Sandra.

It only made sense that somebody could be holding something over Pender also—something like evidence that might get him disbarred.

Were the Shacklefords behind all these crimes? And if they were, what were they hoping to prove or accomplish?

Cassidy didn't know.

But at least she was making progress.

CHAPTER TWENTY-SEVEN

TY FELT a rush of relief when he saw Cassidy walk in the front door.

The storm outside blew a gust of wind into the house, sending Cassidy's hair—which had been released from its bun—in a flurry through the air. Debris hit the house, and Ty knew a good five inches of water filled the lane leading to their cottage. But, all in all, it could be a lot worse.

It was getting late, and Ty had been worried about what might have transpired between Cassidy and Watkins. The fact he hadn't heard from her either meant she was onto something or that the FBI had been giving her a hard time.

But this wasn't the time for them to talk about it either—not with Annabeth listening.

At least, Ty found comfort in the fact that their home hadn't been bugged. He and his guys had checked it out as well as Cassidy's office at the station. Both were clear.

In situations like this, they had to be careful.

"Hey, sweetheart," Cassidy told Annabeth. "Look at these pictures you drew . . . they're beautiful."

Cassidy made more cheerful comments about the pictures Annabeth had been working on. Afterward, they all sat down to eat some baked salmon and potatoes Ty had put together for dinner.

They made generic small talk, keeping things casual.

It wasn't until they tucked the child into bed and went back into the living room and sat beside each other on the couch that they could really talk. Speaking in low tones, Cassidy told Ty what had transpired.

He listened as Cassidy told him about finding Sandra Myers' body and as she recounted what Watkins had revealed about Sandra's job with the FBI.

When Cassidy finished, Ty let out a grunt. "I'm sorry to hear about Sandra. Let's just hope that she was already dead before she went in the water."

"I agree." Cassidy tucked her legs beneath her

and frowned. "It just goes to prove that whoever is behind this is calculated. They carefully planned where to place the body so it wouldn't be discovered."

"Not anticipating that we might have a storm that would mess up everything."

"Exactly." Cassidy swallowed hard and licked her lips. "There's one more thing."

She grabbed her phone and showed Ty the message there.

THAT COULD BE YOU.

TY SUCKED in a breath as concern ricocheted through him. "The person who sent this . . . he was talking about Sandra?"

Grim lines pulled at Cassidy's lips as she frowned. "I can only assume. We'd just found her body."

A sense of foreboding pressed on Ty. This had just moved to the next level of hostile. Someone had basically threatened Cassidy's life. "So someone is watching you?"

"I looked around and didn't see anybody. But

that doesn't mean that someone didn't see us pull down the lane next to Fred's house and put everything together."

Ty sighed. He didn't know what to say—only that he wanted to find the person who was responsible for this and make them pay. It wasn't a very Christian attitude, but he'd be lying to himself if he denied it.

"There's one other thing." Cassidy shifted, settling into the couch further. "The judge halted the custody order for Annabeth. But we may have to appear before him."

Appear before him? Normally that wouldn't be a problem but . . . "Where is this judge?"

"I'm not sure, but he won't be here on Lantern Beach. That's for sure. We'll, at the very least, have to go to the mainland."

Ty shook his head again, unseen burdens pressing on him. "Every time you leave this island, you put yourself at risk."

Cassidy leaned closer and rested her hands on his chest. "I know. Believe me, I know."

Ty ran a hand over his face. He wished things were easier, that the answers were clear. But that was hardly ever the case.

"What are we going to do?" he finally asked.

"We'll cross that bridge when we get there." Cassidy's voice cracked as if she tried to hold back her emotions. "That's the only thing that I know to do."

Ty let out a breath before pulling Cassidy into his arms. That was all he could do. Hold her. Savor her embrace. Love her.

Because sometimes it felt like everything was crumbling around him.

And he couldn't deal with that . . . nor could Ty deal with the thought that there was nothing he could do to fix it.

<hr>

CASSIDY TOSSED and turned in bed, desperate to get some sleep. But her mind wouldn't seem to turn off.

Instead, she reviewed everything that had happened. Yet all of that restlessness did nothing to help her find some answers. She turned over and stared at Ty sleeping beside her.

Except he wasn't sleeping.

He lay in bed facing her, with his eyes open.

She reached forward and ran her hand down his cheek. "You can't sleep either?"

"I can't. I wish I could. I know it would do me a world of good."

"Same here." She beat the pillow beneath her, trying to make it more comfortable, as if the pillow were the problem.

Before they could talk any more, she heard a sound.

Cassidy shot upright in bed, her entire body stiff. Ty pushed himself up also. He'd heard it too.

She tensed as she waited to hear it again.

And she did.

It was a cry.

Then another. And another.

The sound grew with every second that passed.

Wasting no more time, Cassidy and Ty dashed out of bed and rushed across the hall to Annabeth's room.

Had someone broken in? Was the girl okay?

They both paused inside the doorway when they saw Annabeth flinging her arms at the mattress.

"No! No! No!" The girl was having a nightmare.

And she was speaking.

Cassidy exchanged a glance with Ty before quietly approaching the girl's bed. Gently, she sat on the edge of the mattress and put her hand on Annabeth's back. "Annabeth, it's me. Cassidy. It's okay."

She cried out again, and her fist hit the bed. "No!"

Cassidy leaned closer. "Annabeth, it's me. You're okay. You're here with me and Ty."

The next instant, the girl's eyes flung open. After a moment of stunned silence, she broke from her trance-like state and threw herself into Cassidy's arms.

Sobs escaped from her body, the sound seeming to leak from her very soul.

Cassidy held her close, looking over at Ty. They didn't have to say a word to communicate unsaid conversations.

Seeing the girl go through this nightmare was gut-wrenching.

But maybe it was healthy for Annabeth to get this out.

As Cassidy held the girl closer, the only thing she truly wished was that she could take away any pain Annabeth felt.

CHAPTER TWENTY-EIGHT

CASSIDY STOPPED by The Crazy Chefette before work the next morning to grab some coffee and quickly catch up with her friends Lisa and Skye. She was also able to hold Julia and love on the little baby for a few minutes before heading into work.

Those moments of normalcy were so important in order for Cassidy to keep her sanity, especially with the high-profile case she was dealing with now.

But Cassidy also couldn't forget the fact that these people she loved and considered friends could possibly be in danger if the wrong person found out who Cassidy really was.

If this continued to escalate—and she felt sure that it would—she wasn't sure how she would proceed.

As Cassidy had lain in bed last night, she'd thought about what it would be like to pack a few things and leave without telling anyone.

It would be the safest option for her friends.

Safest *physically*, at least.

Emotionally, it would be a different story.

Cassidy knew she couldn't leave Ty like that.

But she hated thinking about the threats he might be facing because of her.

She certainly had a lot to consider. The decisions nagged at her until knots tightened her back and neck muscles.

She shook her head.

Right now, Cassidy needed to think about the crimes happening here on the island. They were a good distraction from her otherwise melancholy thoughts.

She went to the station, muttered hello to several people, and then finally escaped into her office. She set her coffee down on the desk before reading the various notes and messages that had been left for her since she'd been gone overnight.

There were apparently no updates on Sandra. The autopsy was still being performed. Based on what Cassidy had seen, the woman had died of blunt force trauma to the head. She was still waiting for a confirmation on that.

The tire tracks from Seacret Escape matched the ones found at the cottage where Ranger had led them. That came as no surprise.

Just as she finished reviewing that report, Paige stuck her head through the doorway. "Chief, we just got a call from someone who said the distinct scent of weed is coming from his neighbor's house."

"Can you get someone else to handle it?"

"I thought you might want to do it yourself." Paige paused. "The house is located across the street from Seacret Escape."

Cassidy's breath caught. "Is that right?"

Paige nodded as if she understood that the pieces might connect. That's what made her so good at her job and a perfect match for their friend Wes. "It might not be anything . . . but it might be something."

Cassidy stood. "I'll handle this one myself."

CASSIDY KNOCKED at the door to Steve Ricks' place. Even as she stood on his deck, she could smell the distinct scent of pot. In fact, she could smell it when she stepped out of her SUV.

She was surprised she hadn't noticed it when she questioned him earlier in the week. Then again, she remembered smelling fish and candles. Those scents must have been intended to cover any other odors.

Cassidy knocked again, but the man inside—Steve—still didn't answer.

"Police!" Cassidy called. "I know you're in there. Open up!"

Movement sounded inside, and Cassidy wondered if the man might run. She braced herself for either a confrontation or a chase.

Instead, the door opened and the man staying there peeked out, only a fourth of his face showing. "Can I help you?"

Even though the door was only open by two inches, more earthy scents of marijuana drifted out. The scent was unmistakable.

"Police Chief Cassidy Chambers. We had a report about a suspicious smell coming from your house, and I'd like to come inside for a moment."

Steve frowned, his eyes squinty and his words fast. "I'd prefer you didn't."

Perhaps she'd been too nice . . . "Mr. Ricks, we

received a complaint that you're doing drugs inside, and I'm going to need to check things out."

He squinted again until his eyes were barely visible. "I'm minding my own business. That's all I'm doing. Quite frankly, other people would be better off if they adopted that same philosophy."

"You do realize that marijuana is illegal in North Carolina, don't you?"

He paused for a second. "Is it?"

Cassidy resisted a sigh. This guy wasn't going to make this easy, was he? "Look, we can do things the easy way or the hard way. It's your choice."

Steve stared at her another moment before finally opening the door.

A rush of haze escaped, along with an overwhelming woodsy, herbal scent.

Suddenly, some of the man's squirrelly behavior when they'd first spoken made sense—in addition to the overwhelming floral and fish aromas.

"I have a question for you," Cassidy started. "And it's not about your recreational habits."

He eyed her suspiciously as he stood near the entryway, not budging a step farther into the house. "What do you need to know?"

"You were trying to get rid of me the first time I

came by. Now I know why. But I need to know if you saw anyone at the house across the street."

He shrugged. "Who said I saw anything?"

"You're the paranoid type," Cassidy said. "You knew I was coming here to question you. That's why you tried to cover up the scent before I got here. That's why you answered all of my questions as quickly as possible. You wanted to get rid of me. But that doesn't mean you didn't see anything."

The man's eyes widened, and Cassidy knew she had him.

"I was telling you the truth . . . mostly." He shrugged.

Cassidy crossed her arms as she stared the man down. "Tell me the part that you didn't tell me then."

The man swallowed hard and rubbed his throat. "Are you going to press charges for my marijuana?"

"That depends on how helpful you are."

"Okay, okay." He raised his hands in the air as if begging for a little mercy. "I did see one other person over there. I just didn't think it was significant. And you're right. I wanted to get rid of you."

"Who was this person that you saw?"

"I don't know." He shrugged again, his words coming out more quickly. "He drove a truck with some kind of logo on the side, and he carried a brief-case when he walked toward the door."

"Could you describe him?"

Steve let out a deep breath before rubbing his chin. "All I could tell from a distance was that the man had a thick black-and-white beard."

Cassidy sucked in a breath. Like the man from The Crazy Chefette? Not that others on the island didn't have beards, but . . . "Steve, could the logo on his truck have possibly read True View Windows?"

Steve thought about it for a moment before nodding. "You know, I think that's what it was."

Cassidy's back muscles tensed.

It sounded like the same man who'd come to her house and left that brochure. The same man Cassidy had seen in The Crazy Chefette sitting near the FBI agents. Perhaps that had been on purpose?

She didn't know.

But she needed to talk to Ty.

Because maybe the answers had been closer than she thought.

CHAPTER TWENTY-NINE

TY COULD SENSE Annabeth was getting restless. She continuously peered out the window, something close to longing in her gaze.

The day turned out to be beautiful, and it seemed like a shame not to enjoy it. Yesterday's storm had breezed by, leaving mild weather in its wake.

"You want to go outside, don't you?" Ty asked Annabeth.

She turned toward him, her eyes bright at his suggestion.

He thought about it another moment, weighing the risks, before finally nodding.

"Okay, then," Ty finally said. "Put some shoes on."

As she did that, Ty made sure his gun was loaded. A few minutes later, they stepped outside.

Leaving the safety of the house, Ty couldn't stop thinking about the photos that had been sent to him, the ones of him and Annabeth and Kujo walking down the shoreline. He knew it was a good possibility that somebody was still watching them.

That meant that he needed to be even more vigilant than he'd been before.

But the one thing Ty didn't want to do was to hide.

Before he walked down the steps, he scanned the landscape around him. The lane leading to his place. The marsh grass on the other side of the cottage. The ocean out front.

No one was out here at this end of the beach. During tourist season, the sandy shores would fill up more. But at this time of the year, Ty practically had the place to himself.

Kujo ran ahead of them to the beach, no doubt looking for birds or crabs to chase.

Annabeth took Ty's hand and practically skipped as she climbed the sand dune.

Ty paused as they reached the top. He glanced around again, looking for anybody who might be watching.

He saw no one.

With that reassurance, he smiled down at Annabeth. "Let's go explore!"

The two of them began walking close to the ocean. The sound of the waves obscured the sound of any footsteps. That meant he needed to be extra cautious.

But it felt good to be outside and breathe some fresh air.

Annabeth certainly enjoyed it. She smiled and twirled and chased waves.

The sight of it made him smile.

They climbed closer to the shore as the beach became more narrow.

Again, Ty looked around but saw nothing.

Kujo seemed at ease as he enjoyed the beach. If the dog sensed someone nearby, he would at least look in their direction. But instead, he focused on the shoreline and the crabs he could find.

Reassured, Ty decided they would go a little farther before they turned around and made their way back to the cottage.

As they walked, Ty's phone buzzed.

He pulled it from his pocket and glanced at the screen.

When he did, he saw he'd gotten another message from that same unknown number.

Trepidation filled him as he clicked on the photos that had been sent.

But this time, they weren't of him and Annabeth on the beach.

No, this time they were pictures of Cassidy— only the photos weren't recent.

They were pictures of Cassidy . . . from when she'd been a detective in Seattle and had gone by Cady Matthews.

WHILE CASSIDY SAT in her SUV on the street near Steve's place, she pulled out her phone and did some more research on True View Windows.

She was surprised when she pulled up the company's home page to see a picture of a man with a full black-and-white beard on the front.

He was listed as the founder and owner of the business, somebody named Rob Freeman.

This was the same guy she'd seen in The Crazy Chefette.

But why would the president and CEO of the

company go door to door himself in a small town like Lantern Beach trying to drum up business?

Unless it was a startup company.

Cassidy continued to research the business, only to discover that True View was a national company with multiple offices and locations.

This was no small-time operation.

That only made her questions grow even more.

Something was wrong.

Either this man wasn't who he said he was . . . or he was up to something.

Cassidy hadn't gotten a good enough look at him to know for sure.

But a bad feeling rumbled in her stomach.

Right now, she wanted to talk to Ty. Get his feedback. Warn him.

She put her SUV in Drive.

Something told her she didn't have any time to waste.

CHAPTER THIRTY

TY PULLED his gaze away from the picture, which had sent him into momentary shock.

When he did, he noticed that Annabeth was no longer right beside him.

A surge of panic rushed through him as he glanced around.

Where had she gone? Ty knew the girl was quick, but she usually stayed close.

Finally, he spotted Annabeth in the distance, climbing a sand dune.

A kite appeared to be stuck in the grass there, and the girl reached for it.

It seemed harmless enough, but Ty still didn't like her being that far away from him.

"Annabeth!" Ty yelled.

But the girl hardly looked at him. Maybe she couldn't hear him over the waves.

He picked up his pace into a jog. "Annabeth!"

In the distance, Annabeth reached for the kite, trying to untangle the string from the sea oats.

As Ty moved toward her, he glanced around. There was still nobody on the beach. Nobody in the distance even.

But just as that thought crossed his mind, a man appeared over the dune.

Only a few feet away from Annabeth.

Another surge of worry rushed through Ty.

Especially when he recognized the man.

It was the guy who'd been selling windows around town.

And he was walking straight toward Annabeth.

Ty reached for the gun at his waistband, knowing he needed to be prepared for the worst.

"TY? ANNABETH?"

Cassidy scanned the inside of her home with its beige and teal colors. There were no signs of life.

Concern pulsed through her.

Where could Ty and Annabeth have gone? Kujo wasn't here either.

They must have gone for a walk, Cassidy realized. It was the only explanation that made sense, especially since Ty's truck was still parked at the house.

Cassidy charged from the house and climbed over the dune.

She wasn't sure why she felt such an urgent need to show Ty this picture. But she did.

In her gut, she could feel they were closing in on whoever was behind this and getting closer to finding answers.

But the closer they came to answers, the more danger they were all in.

She had no doubt about that.

She paused on the other side of the dune. As she scanned the shoreline, she spotted three figures in the distance.

Three figures? Who was the third one?

She sucked in a breath as the truth washed over her.

It was the man with the salt-and-pepper beard. The one she'd seen in The Crazy Chefette.

He stood near Ty and Annabeth.

A wave of urgency crashed on Cassidy.

She darted across the sand, desperate to get to them in time to help in case things went south.

Was this man trying to abduct Annabeth? The thought made anger simmer in her blood.

She knew Ty could handle himself. But that didn't mean that she liked this situation. Not one bit.

"Police!" Cassidy yelled as she darted toward the scene.

As soon as the bearded man saw her, he threw his hands in the air and stepped back.

This man wasn't going to get away.

Cassidy would get some answers from him . . . one way or another.

CHAPTER THIRTY-ONE

AS CASSIDY DREW HER WEAPON, Ty pushed Annabeth behind him and stepped back.

"I think we have a misunderstanding here." The man's eyes widened and darted around as if he were near panic.

Sensing the rising tension, Kujo came to guard Annabeth, fur bristling in a protective manner.

Cassidy's jaw hardened as she said, "I'll be the judge of that."

The man raised his hands higher, sweat appearing on his forehead. "I can explain. Really. Please."

"Why are you here?" Cassidy held her gun toward the man.

"The girl needed help with her kite. I just happened to be nearby." His voice wavered.

"Stop giving me excuses. What's your real name, and what are you really doing on this island?" Cassidy wasn't going to let him get away with this so easily.

"My name is Rob, just like I've told people. I'm with True View Windows."

"You're the president of the company." Cassidy paused three feet in front of him. "The president of a successful business like yours doesn't go door to door trying to drum up sales. So what are you really doing here?"

His gaze shifted, as if he tried to think of an excuse now that he'd been caught. "I just wanted to get back to those grassroot efforts."

"You went to the house of a woman who later turned up dead. No one else was seen going to see her. No one but you. Do you expect me to believe that was a coincidence?"

"What?" The man's face went paler. "I didn't have anything to do with that. I didn't even know . . . Please. You've got to believe me."

Cassidy's voice remained hard. "We need to talk. Now."

The man nodded quickly—not bothering to

hide his desperation. "Of course. Anything you need. But I was never going to hurt anybody. I promise."

TY KEPT a hand on Rob's arm as he led the man to the cottage. Meanwhile, Cassidy walked with Annabeth and Kujo, no doubt keeping an eye on the situation in front of her. Right now, she was a mix of cop and mom—a dangerous combination if Ty had ever seen one.

Who was this man really? What did Cassidy know that Ty didn't?

He hoped to find out those answers soon.

Ty led the man back to the house, neither of them saying anything. As soon as they were inside, Cassidy took Annabeth to her room and instructed her to stay there with Kujo for a few minutes.

Cassidy's jaw was almost as hard as her eyes when she returned.

Ty nudged Rob into a dining room chair while both he and Cassidy stood in front of him.

They were dealing with a killer here on this island—a killer who had murdered a federal agent.

This was no time to play nice.

"Who are you really?" Cassidy demanded, her eyes narrow with focus.

"I told you." The man's words came out fast, heightened. "My name is Rob. Rob Freeman."

"What are you doing here on this island?" Cassidy pushed. "And don't tell me you're trying to sell windows."

The man opened his mouth but then shut it again as if thinking twice about what he was going to say. His foot shook beneath the table, practically causing a tremor throughout the whole room.

"Someone challenged me that I should get out here and try to sell windows myself," he blurted. "So that's what I'm doing."

"Who exactly challenged you to do that?" Cassidy demanded.

"It's a long story."

Cassidy crossed her arms. "We have time. Besides, we're searching for a killer on this island, and right now you are at the top of my suspect list."

The man's eyes widened until Ty saw the whites all around his pupils. "I didn't kill anybody. You've got the wrong guy."

Cassidy narrowed her gaze. "Then why did you pay a visit to our murder victim?"

"Because someone told me to go to that address!"

As soon as Rob said the words, he lowered his head and buried his face in his hands.

Cassidy twisted her neck, still not letting up. "You're going to need to explain that a little bit more."

Even as Cassidy said those words, a theory began to brew in Ty's mind.

He stepped back, anxious to see if he was correct. Because, if he was, his theory might answer a lot of questions.

CHAPTER THIRTY-TWO

CASSIDY EYED the man in front of her, her muscles bristling and ready for action. She couldn't trust this man yet. He obviously had ulterior motives—and he'd approached Annabeth. That automatically put him on Cassidy's bad list.

She crossed her arms as she addressed him. "I'm listening."

She couldn't imagine what he might have to say.

The man raised his head and arms again. "If I tell you something, can we keep it between us?"

"That depends on what you tell me."

Rob's neck muscles tightened, and he rubbed his throat, almost as if he couldn't breathe. "If the wrong person finds out, I'll be a dead man."

Cassidy narrowed her gaze, not in the mood to

placate anyone. The stakes were too high. "If discretion is warranted, then you'll have it."

The man licked his lips before quickly nodding in short, jerky motions. "Fine. I got a text message about six days ago that instructed me to come to Lantern Beach where I would receive further instructions. If I didn't, someone was going to reveal one of my secrets."

Cassidy sucked in a breath. The same man who'd been threatening various people had also threatened this guy. That's what she'd been afraid of.

"Exactly what kind of secret is this guy holding against you?" she asked.

Rob shook his head, the look in his gaze one of pure agony and desperation. "Please. Don't make me tell you."

"I know you don't want to share, but, if it's not relevant to this investigation, it won't matter."

Rob hung his head again and remained silent for several minutes until he finally said, "I've gotten deep into some debt because of a . . . gambling addiction. If my wife finds out about it, she'll leave me. And if the board of directors for my company finds out about it . . . I'll most likely lose my business."

"Those are pretty high stakes," Cassidy said.

Rob nodded, but his eyes looked hollow. "Believe me, I know. That's why I don't want anyone to find out. So, of course, I decided to come here instead."

Ty stepped closer, his broad form an intimidating figure as he stood beside Cassidy. "What instructions did you receive after you arrived?"

Rob rubbed his throat again. "I was sent a list of addresses and instructed to go to each one to try to sell people windows. That was it. The directions were pretty simple. Even though they didn't make sense to me, I was glad that was all this person asked of me."

Someone had been trying to frame him, Cassidy realized. They'd sent this guy to all the places where the killer might have been.

Somebody must have known that people would become suspicious of Rob.

Whoever was behind these crimes was clever, Cassidy realized. Too clever. Too calculated.

"Did this person send you over here today?" Ty glowered down at the man. "Or was it really a coincidence you ran into us?"

"I got a text message saying to come back here and follow up about those windows," Rob rushed. "But when I arrived, I saw you walking down the beach. That's when I decided to try to make it look casual."

"I'm going to need to see those text messages," Cassidy said. "If there are any more addresses on your list, I need to know about them also." Who else could this person be targeting?

"Of course. Anything you need. You've just got to believe me when I say I would never hurt somebody. Never."

In any other circumstance, Cassidy may not believe him.

But considering the fact that she'd received those same threats, she knew he was most likely telling the truth.

Someone had just wasted a whole lot of her time.

But the question was still who.

CASSIDY LET ROB GO, but he promised to update her if he got any more text messages. She had no good reason to keep him. In fact, he might be better off if he waited for further instructions.

Whoever was behind this was going to slip up sometime. Cassidy needed to be there when he did.

Ty started a pot of coffee after the man left and

then the two of them sat down to talk. They'd gone to check on Annabeth, and the girl had seemed surprisingly unconcerned. She'd found some blocks and begun building a tower in her room, content to play alone.

Cassidy turned to him, exhaustion wrinkling the corners of her eyes. "This just keeps getting bigger and bigger, doesn't it?"

"When I saw Rob's face, I suspected his motive might be something like this." Ty shook his head. "Someone has a whole crime ring based on threats to reveal people's secrets and sins. How are they learning this information? And what do the people behind these threats get out of this? That's what I can't figure out."

Cassidy leaned back. Revealing people's sins? When it was worded like that . . . it made her skin crawl. But Ty's assessment was accurate.

"I've been thinking about that also, and I can't figure it out either. Is it the satisfaction of being in control?"

"This is a lot of trouble to go through just for someone to be entertained." Ty rose and grabbed two mugs of coffee before handing Cassidy one and sitting at the dining room table beside her.

"I agree," Cassidy said. "Then what? I'd say

maybe they're trying to bring down people in power. But I'm a small-town police chief. What could they possibly want to prove by bringing me down?"

"If they know your real identity, maybe they want to somehow get to your parents."

Cassidy frowned. "I suppose it's a possibility. But what about this Rob guy? Sure, he owns that company. But I have trouble seeing how the pieces fit. I think once we know the motive of the perp behind this, then we'll have a lot of answers we need."

Ty took a sip of his coffee. "I agree. I'm just glad that this guy didn't try to hurt Annabeth."

Cassidy glanced up at him, still processing what had just happened. "I'm surprised you let him get that close."

"A few minutes before that, I got a text message."

Cassidy's spine straightened. "What kind of message?"

He pulled out his phone and showed her the pictures.

Cassidy's breath caught. In the photos, she had straight dark hair. She'd had to change her hair when she had come here so nobody would recognize her. Now, every three weeks, she bleached her roots.

Instead of straightening her naturally wavy hair, she used products to enhance the curl and the wave.

Looking at the picture reminded Cassidy of who she'd been at one time. Sometimes, that person seemed like a ghost. It seemed like she'd lived another life.

That's probably because she had.

"So the person making these threats obviously knows what they're talking about." Cassidy's throat felt raw and scratchy as the words left her lips. "I don't like this, Ty."

He reached across the table and squeezed her hands. "I don't like it either."

Just then, her phone buzzed. Dread pooled in her stomach.

As she glanced at the screen, stark words stared back.

BRING **us $100,000 or your identity will be revealed. More instructions are coming.**

IT LOOKED like she may have found her motive.

Money.

CHAPTER THIRTY-THREE

TY GLANCED at his watch and frowned. He hated to wrap up this conversation—especially considering the threat Cassidy had just received. But it looked like he had no choice. They'd have more time to talk later.

"I told Sami she could meet with Annabeth again in twenty minutes," he started. "I nearly forgot except my phone sent me a reminder. Should I reschedule?"

"No." Cassidy rose and put her coffee mug in the sink. "It's important that Annabeth gets the attention she needs. I feel like she and Sami made some good progress last time."

"I agree." Ty stood from the table. "I'll go get her now."

"I'd like to come with you," Cassidy said. "I can probably only stay for a few minutes until I have to get back to work but . . ."

"Of course. I'd like that."

Several minutes later, Ty and Annabeth were in his truck headed toward the Blackout complex. Cassidy drove separately in case she needed to leave, which she probably would. But Ty was glad she'd be there for at least part of this.

Ty couldn't stop thinking about that $100,000.

They didn't have that kind of money.

Cassidy's parents could get that amount in the blink of an eye. Not that Ty had ever met them. Or that they'd ever been here. But he knew enough from talking to Cassidy to know that money was never a problem for them.

Was the person who'd sent that text bluffing? Or would they really expose Cassidy unless she paid up?

If Ty's hunch was correct, everyone else this person had been threatening would soon be getting the same kind of text. These people had had their fun, and now they wanted a payoff for it. A payoff bigger than the satisfaction of making other people suffer for their past actions.

Cassidy had said that they couldn't pay. Had said that the extortionist would just take the hush money and demand more. That the process would be ongoing.

Ty had seen a haunted look in his wife's eyes, and he prayed Cassidy wasn't thinking about doing anything drastic.

Because he knew Cassidy. He knew that she'd do whatever necessary to keep the people she loved safe.

He pulled up to Blackout, put his truck in Park, and then waited for Cassidy to join him before going inside.

As soon as they stepped into the lobby, Ty spotted Elise and Bethany talking in the distance. Based on the wide grins on their faces, they had good news.

The women saw Ty, Cassidy, and Annabeth at the same time and hurried over to them.

Cassidy stopped near the women and eyed them. "You both look like the cat who ate the canary."

"We have good news," Elise said. "I wanted to wait and have a party to announce it. But I'm not patient enough to do that."

"What's going on?" Ty asked.

Elise and Bethany grabbed each other's hands. As they turned back to Ty and Cassidy, they announced, "We're both pregnant!"

EVERYTHING WENT STILL around Cassidy at her friends' words.

Just as quickly, she snapped back to reality and plastered on a smile.

"What? That's great. Congratulations, you guys." Without missing a beat, Cassidy stepped toward them and pulled them both into a hug. "I'm so happy for you."

Ty hugged them also and offered his congratulations.

"When are you both due?" Cassidy tried to keep the tremble from her voice.

"In seven months," Bethany said.

"And I'm due in six and a half," Elise said. "I've been sitting on the news, trying to wait until my first trimester was over. But then I heard Bethany's news, and that was that."

"I'm sure Colton and Griff are thrilled, as is Ada," Ty said.

"They're *so* excited," Bethany said. "We may have

to start our own little school here on the Blackout campus before too long."

"We may have to do that." Ty smiled. "I look forward to celebrating with you guys when we have the chance. We'll have you all over for dinner soon."

"We'd love that." Elise's eyes softened as she glanced at Cassidy.

Did she sense the grief Cassidy felt at the news? As a psychologist, the woman was intuitive.

But Cassidy didn't want to do anything to take away the joy of their announcement.

She plastered on another smile as she stepped toward the hallway. "We'll talk more later, ladies. Congratulations again."

Cassidy, Ty, and Annabeth continued down the hallway to find Sami.

Cassidy wished she was truly happy for her friends. No, she *was* happy for them. She wanted only the best for those ladies and their families. The best was what they deserved.

But Cassidy dreamed about the day when she could share that same kind of news.

It looked like it probably wouldn't ever happen.

That thought made sadness press on her until she could hardly breathe.

When would this pain ease?

Or would it?

Cassidy didn't know.

CHAPTER THIRTY-FOUR

AS ANNABETH and Sami went into the conference room together, Ty turned to Cassidy. "Are you doing okay?"

Although he knew Cassidy was truly happy for their friends, Ty also knew that news had to be hard to hear.

She nodded, even though her gaze seemed almost glazed. "I'm really happy for them."

Ty squeezed her arm. "I know you are. But I also know that couldn't have been easy for you."

"I guess it's hard to realize that your dreams may never happen."

"Don't say that," he whispered. "We don't know what's going to happen."

Cassidy shook her head. "Even if we were able to

have a child, it would be a bad idea to bring one into this world."

His spine stiffened as he tried to read between the lines of what she was saying. "What do you mean?"

"Just like we've talked about before," Cassidy said. "As long as DH-7 is still in existence, I'm always going to be in danger. As long as terrorists and insurgents know you were a part of the SEAL team that brought their regime down, you're still going to be in danger. Our lives are never going to be normal. It would be irresponsible to bring a child into a situation like this."

"Cassidy . . ." Ty tried to find the right words. "I know where you're coming from. But everybody in this world has things that could hold them back. The important thing is believing that we can overcome."

"But when does trying to overcome something really equate to being selfish? Because bringing a child into a dangerous world seems like a terrible idea for the child. Maybe that's what God's trying to tell us."

Ty opened his mouth and then shut it. Again, he struggled to know what to say. Because on one hand,

Cassidy was right. But on the other hand, he knew that the situation wasn't that simple.

And still, the fact remained that the doctor had said Ty and Cassidy probably weren't physically going to be able to have children on their own.

Almost as if reading his thoughts, Cassidy shrugged. "Besides, me leaving this island right now for something like in vitro is a terrible idea. I need to stay put and keep a low profile. It's hard enough dealing with all the crimes popping up here on the island. I certainly don't need to make it any easier for these guys who might come after me."

Her words sounded strong, but Ty heard the grief behind them. "We could try to come up with the hundred grand, Cassidy. Are you sure you don't want to?"

Ty knew his words were borne of desperation. In any other circumstances, he wouldn't have even suggested it. But he'd do anything to keep Cassidy safe.

Anything.

As Cassidy looked up at him, he saw something else in her gaze.

What was that?

CASSIDY LICKED her lips and swallowed. She'd already told Ty that if they gave this person money, the perp would only ask for more. They would forever be in this person's clutches.

And that was no way to live.

Which had brought her to another idea.

What if Cassidy were to step forward and admit to the world Cady Matthews was still alive? To beat these guys to the punch? That way they'd have nothing to hold over her.

But she didn't know what it would prove either. If everyone in DH-7 knew she was alive, she'd still be in the same situation. She'd still always be hiding, waiting for someone else to find her.

And sometimes she was so tired of hiding.

On occasion, Cassidy scanned the web for any articles of interest on DH-7. From what she'd read, the gang's influence seemed to be waning. She hoped that one day, the organization might dissolve.

But she also knew that was most likely wishful thinking.

Cassidy shrugged and her attention turned back to Ty. "We can't pay the money. It goes against everything I believe in."

"So we just wait for them to act?" Ty studied her

face, as if trying to get a pulse on the situation—and on Cassidy's feelings.

"I'm trying to think of a solution." DH-7 was big with members clustered across several states. It was too big to take down. Many law enforcement agencies had tried.

"I know you're trying to figure this out. So am I. But we're going to need to explore every option here."

Cassidy nodded, even though part of her almost felt numb.

Numb because she knew there wasn't any good solution.

But she didn't know how to tell Ty that.

As her phone rang, she saw a number she hadn't seen in a long time. She frowned before putting the device to her ear. "Stephens?"

Samuel Stephens was the FBI agent who helped her fake her own death in order to free her from being hunted by DH-7. She hadn't talked to him in at least a year.

"Lantern Beach popped up during my debriefing," he said, getting right to the point.

"Did it?" She had no idea where he was going with this, but it couldn't be anywhere good.

"I saw that Special Agent Donald Watkins was

there investigating the death of Special Agent Sandra Myers."

"That's correct."

"I don't know how to tell you this, Cassidy, but be careful around him."

Her spine stiffened. "What do you mean?"

"I mean, I worked with him for a year in DC, and there's something about him I don't trust. I never found anything concrete to confirm my suspicions. But I don't like the fact that he's anywhere near you."

"In other words, don't trust him."

"No, definitely don't trust him. If I learn anything irrefutable, I'll let you know."

"Got it."

"How is everything?"

How did Cassidy even answer that? "To be honest, it's not great."

CHAPTER THIRTY-FIVE

"I'VE GOT GOOD NEWS." Sami's cheerful voice pulled Cassidy and Ty from the otherwise dark moment.

Cassidy glanced up from where she talked to Ty in the conference room. She shoved aside thoughts of her conversation with Samuel and turned her full attention on the ever-friendly, ever-cheerful Sami.

"We always like good news." Ty slipped his arm around Cassidy's waist as they waited to hear what she had to say.

"Annabeth is making real progress." Sami paused in front of them, casting a warm glance back at Annabeth, who still played in a little room off the main conference area. "I tried to get her to say a few things, and she moved her mouth. I think she wants to speak again. It's just getting over the hurdle of doing it for the first time."

"I'm glad she's making some progress," Cassidy said. "She did have a nightmare where she shouted 'no' last night. I thought I should mention that. I can't be sure, but it may have even been a night terror."

Sami frowned before nodding. "That would be perfectly normal in a situation like this. It's her subconscious way of trying to work out everything that's happened. Speaking of which, are there any updates on her parents?"

"Her dad is still in a coma, and her mom is still missing. Someone stepped up, out of the blue, to claim legal guardianship of her. The paperwork looks legit, but with a few questionable phrases, and a judge is looking it over. I'm afraid that the legal system is going to try to take her away from us before it's time." Cassidy's voice cracked as she finished the update, and she rubbed her throat, almost as if it were sore.

Sami frowned before shaking her head. "That would be a really bad idea. Annabeth obviously feels safe with the two of you. Being thrust into a new situation like that would only slow her healing process."

"If it comes down to it, would you be willing to speak on her behalf?" Ty asked.

Sami nodded, no hints of hesitation in her body language. "Of course. Anything I can do to help. I want whatever is in the child's best interest, and I think the two of you are what Annabeth needs right now. When she looks at you, her eyes practically glow."

Cassidy glanced at Annabeth again as the girl colored something at the table. She was so glad the girl felt secure with her.

Could this child be the answer to her prayers? Or would staying with Ty and Cassidy only put Annabeth in more danger?

CASSIDY LEFT Ty and Annabeth at the Blackout complex and went back to the station.

She tried to get her conversation with Sami out of her head and focus on her work. But it was hard.

Just like it was hard to forget about the demand for money.

There were no good solutions. But Cassidy only had a day left to figure things out according to the verbal agreement between her and Hollick.

Pressure continued to knot Cassidy's shoulders until her neck hurt.

Just as she poured her last cup of coffee, her phone rang. "Police Chief Cassidy Chambers."

"Chief Chambers, this is Mindy Broderick. I work for social services in Winchester, Virginia."

As soon as Cassidy heard "social services," a rush of panic went through her. Then she realized this wasn't about Annabeth.

A couple of days ago, Cassidy had put in a call to the social worker who was associated with Alexandria Manchester after her parents had died.

"I appreciate you taking the time to call me back," Cassidy started. "I'm working a case, and I was hoping that you could answer a few questions for me."

"Who's the case pertaining to?"

"Someone named Alexandria Manchester."

"I'm afraid that name doesn't sound familiar."

Cassidy stiffened. Mindy's name had popped up when Cassidy had done her research. "Her maiden name was Morris. Alexandria Morris. Does that ring any bells?"

The social worker let out a long *hmm*. "I *did* have a girl I worked with named Alexis Morris. Could it be the same person?"

"I'm not sure. I haven't heard that name before. But anything is a possibility."

"Let me pull out my files. But if this is the girl that I'm thinking it is, you're going to want to be sitting down."

Cassidy tensed.

Maybe this was the lead she'd been looking—and praying—to find.

CHAPTER THIRTY-SIX

"I GUESSED CORRECTLY." Satisfaction rang through the social worker's voice. "But I need to be certain I can share this information."

"Alexandria Morris' life is in danger," Cassidy said. "Whatever is said won't lead back to you. But it's urgent that I know anything that might help me find her."

"Understood. Of course, I want to help." Mindy paused as if gathering her thoughts. Finally, she said, "Alexis Morris and Alexandria Morris are the same person. She changed her name legally for a brief period of time."

Cassidy let Mindy's words sink in. "Why would she do that?"

"Alexis was always a troubled girl. It's understandable when you consider the trauma she went through."

The woman had Cassidy's full attention now. "What kind of trauma was that?"

"The poor girl was shuffled from foster care family to foster care family for the longest time. Often times, kids in these situations look for somewhere they can belong, often a group of friends, and Alexis was no different."

"Go on."

"She always had exceptional computer skills. She probably got them from her father, who owned his own IT business before he was killed. Unfortunately, Alexis did *not* put those talents to good use. She used them to hack into websites."

Cassidy's mind raced as she wondered where this conversation would go. "What do you mean?"

"You said this is just between you and me, right?"

"If I share any of this information with my colleagues, I won't mention your name. I'll be discreet."

Mindy hesitated another moment. "At first, what Alexis did was relatively innocent. I mean, as innocent as anything illegal might be. Alexis would hack into websites in order to get herself a bit of extra money."

"Really?" That had been the last thing Cassidy expected to hear.

"Really. But then it turned into something bigger. Alexis hacked into the school website to change her grades. Her classmates paid Alexis to change their grades as well. It was quite the side hustle she had going on."

"Why was none of this in her records?"

"You didn't hear this from me, but her records may or may not have been sealed. Alexis was a juvenile and went to jail for two years. When she was released, she changed her name back to the designation her parents had given her, and she started a new life."

That wasn't something Cassidy had been expecting to hear. "That explains a lot. When was the last time you spoke with her?"

Mindy let out another sigh as if trying to recall her memories. "Alexis aged out of the foster care system at eighteen. My understanding is that, shortly after, she met the man who's now her husband."

"Dr. Joe Manchester?"

"Yes! He's the one. She seemed to have turned her life around, last I heard." Mindy paused. "You mentioned her life is in danger? What's going on?"

Cassidy nibbled on her bottom lip a moment

before saying, "That's what we're trying to figure out."

"If there's anything else that I can do for you, let me know."

"Will do."

But as Cassidy ended the call, she leaned back in her chair.

Alexandria was a hacker.

Whoever was finding out these secrets about various people was also probably a hacker.

Was Alexandria working with the Shacklefords? Had she masterminded this whole thing? What if she wasn't a victim but an accomplice?

Cassidy had no idea what the answers were.

But as more of her questions were beginning to be answered she didn't like the picture that was forming.

CASSIDY CALLED an emergency meeting of the two people she trusted the most in this world: Ty and Mac.

They met at her office, and Cassidy shared what she'd just learned about Alexandria Manchester.

"Well, I'll be a blue-nosed gopher." Mac shook his head. "This is . . . multi-faceted, to say the least."

"I know." Cassidy glanced at Mac then Ty. "Believe me, I know. That's why I need the two of you here. I need your knowledge and expertise. And I need people who will look at this from a different perspective than I am. What are your thoughts on the situation?"

Ty leaned forward, his intelligent gaze flickering with thought. "I guess the first question that came to my mind is whether or not Alexandria is being forced to do these things or if she is doing them at will."

"I wondered about that too," Cassidy said. "We won't really have a good answer to that until we find Alexandria herself."

"The idea that Alexandria could be involved—and working for the other side—isn't something we really considered, now, is it?" Mac sucked in his cheek in thought. "Maybe she doesn't want to be found. Maybe her abduction was all a ruse."

"That might be true, but this is where it gets muddy to me." Cassidy found herself clicking her ballpoint pen and set it on the table before she drove herself crazy. "Based on everything I've heard,

Alexandria is a loving mother. I have a hard time imagining her putting her child in danger like this."

"People have done stranger, crazier things," Ty said. "When people really believe in a cause, they don't let anything stop them. Believe me, I thought that time and time again in the Middle East and with the insurgents there. I don't want to think that Annabeth's mom is one of those people who'd put a personal vendetta before the safety of her own child. But we'd be foolish not to consider it."

"I agree," Mac said. "It's a possibility that Alexandria was in cahoots with someone else this whole time."

Cassidy nodded, unable to argue with that point. "I wish I didn't have to consider that, but, yes, you're correct."

Mac sighed and shifted in his seat. "Let's also look at the other side of this. Maybe these crimes *do* go back to the Shacklefords. Maybe they're *forcing* Alexandria to do these things. They could be threatening to hurt Annabeth."

"But Annabeth is safe . . ." Ty said.

Cassidy tapped her desk with her finger as she cast a glance at Ty. "But Alexandria might not know that."

Ty tilted his head back and forth as he considered it. "That's true. Either way, the bottom line is that we need to figure out where Alexandria is."

Mac turned back to Cassidy. "I assume you've tried to trace the phone number of the person who's been calling you."

Cassidy nodded as she glanced at the phone on her desk and remembered those messages. "I have. I've had no luck. The messages have been too fast, too short. You know the drill."

"What about tracing the IP addresses of the computers from where some of those messages originated?" Ty asked. "If somebody is hacking into various peoples' records, maybe somebody with cyber security experience can trace them."

"I thought about that," Cassidy said. "But finding the right person to do it for me could expose everyone's secrets—including mine. I'm not sure it's a good idea."

Even if she could trust Watkins, it was risky to talk to the FBI. Then she'd have to open up about the governor and her own secrets. It was too risky. Besides, it was anybody's guess at this point who else was involved. Maybe the threats that Cassidy and the others had received were just the tip of the iceberg.

Mac leaned back in his seat, a deep frown

tugging at his lips. "I think there's one thing we can agree on. Whoever is doing this has to be close. If they sent you a message yesterday saying that dead Sandra Myers could be you, they're obviously near enough to watch."

Cassidy shivered at the reminder. "That seems to be the case. It's not like we're in an area where there are security cameras on every corner. If someone saw me, it was most likely because they were physically watching."

"If they're close, we need to draw them out of their rabbit hole," Mac said. "Do a little shock and awe treatment on them."

"Remind me what that means." Cassidy wanted to make sure they were on the same page.

"Shock and awe is when you surround your enemy and overwhelm them so they have no choice but to give up," Ty answered. "It's a classic military strategy."

Cassidy tried to figure out how they could apply that to this situation. In theory, it sounded great. But she needed a concrete plan.

"You think that's what we should do? Try to draw them out and into a situation where they have no choice but to give up?"

Mac looked at Ty, almost as if volleying the question to him.

"I think that's what these people are doing to the victims they're targeting. They overwhelm them with information and threats until their victims are nearly paralyzed." Ty shrugged. "Maybe we should give them some of their own medicine."

"I love that idea," Cassidy said. "I just can't see how we can make that operational here."

"If these people are staying nearby, they're going to need supplies," Mac said. "They can't simply stay in the area for an extended period of time without getting food. Without paying some type of bill. There are ways to find them."

Ty leaned forward. "I might have an idea."

Cassidy sucked in a breath as she waited to hear what he had to say.

CHAPTER THIRTY-SEVEN

TY SWALLOWED hard before launching into his idea. He didn't want to ever suggest something that put Cassidy in danger. But every investigation required some risk.

He hoped they'd be able to separate the two.

"These people obviously thrive on the internet," he began. "That's how they're finding out this information. Right?"

Cassidy and Mac nodded.

"We're already surrounded by water—a natural boundary," Ty said. "So we cut them off from everything but this island so they have no means of getting away."

Cassidy's intense gaze met his. "First, we need to find them, though."

"The Shacklefords—let's assume they're involved —aren't the type who are going to cook meals for themselves every day. They seem more like the type who would order out, don't they?"

"They do." Cassidy nodded.

"What if we check with local restaurants to see who's been ordering meals to go, and at the general store to see if anyone has placed delivery orders?" Ty suggested. "That seems like the most logical way these people would be getting their food and/or supplies."

Mac nodded. "You may be onto something."

Cassidy didn't say anything for a moment until nodding also. "It's simple, but it might work. You're right. They have to be getting supplies somehow. Someone could be bringing them food, driving it over on the ferry."

"My gut feeling is that this is a simple operation," Ty said. "Probably just the Shacklefords and Alexandria. I'm not sure if they're going to want to involve anyone else. The bigger their circle, the more likely they'll be found out."

Cassidy shifted. "Just one more question. Do we involve the FBI in this? The Coast Guard?"

Ty locked gazes with her. "It's your call. But if we

involve them, there's a chance that all these secrets will come out—including your own secrets."

Cassidy frowned and nodded. "You're right."

"Do you really think this will work?" Mac asked. "Can anybody think of a better plan?"

The three of them glanced at each other. They each knew the truth. There wasn't a better plan.

Just then, Mac's phone buzzed. He grunted before raising the screen.

"It looks like the FBI just released information on the death of Sandra Myers," Mac said. "This is becoming more and more public by the moment. That means we need to move even more quickly."

CASSIDY ENDED her phone call and leaned back in her chair. She'd called most of the stores here on the island, and nobody had shared anything that would help her. Ty, in the meantime, was working on the list of restaurants.

All of this had seemed like a good idea, but what if it was a wild goose chase?

The whole situation made her uncomfortable.

As did the fact that the clock was ticking. She

knew she didn't have a lot of time to figure out what to do.

Her mind drifted back to Ty and Annabeth again. She hated the fact that being near them put them in danger. She would never be able to live with herself if something happened to them because of her. She had to fix the situation. One way or another.

Tension pressed down on her at the thought of it.

She pulled out some Tylenol from her drawer and took a pill, trying to ease the pounding headache pulsing through her.

If she didn't figure out a better way to manage her stress, then she had no doubt she would feel the consequences of that physically. She didn't know what it would take to reduce her stress. Talking to Elise? Taking more time off work? Maybe she should start jogging again to see if that would burn off some of the constant tension.

Of course, none of that would matter if they didn't get through this right now.

Someone stepped into her office, and she looked up. It was Ty.

His eyes looked different, brighter. Maybe he had discovered something.

"So I just talked to someone down at Waterman's," Ty said. "First, they told me they weren't doing any type of deliveries. But then I remembered someone who works as a line cook there, and I gave him a call. It turns out they're making an exception for one person here on the island, only because this person is paying a huge tip for their silence."

Cassidy sat up straighter. "What else did he say?"

"That they're taking dinner to somebody here on the island every evening. This person calls the restaurant manager directly, places the order, and then Tommy Jones delivers it."

Tommy Jones? Cassidy vaguely remembered meeting the teenager.

She glanced at her watch. "So that means in approximately four hours, they may be making a delivery there again?"

Ty nodded. "That's right."

"But the only two people who are supposed to know about this are the manager and Tommy? Even though your friend obviously knows about it also."

"That's my understanding."

"We have four hours to make this work."

"We have a lot of planning and coordinating to do in that time."

Cassidy rose to her feet. "Then we better get busy."

CHAPTER THIRTY-EIGHT

TY KNEW he couldn't risk visiting Tommy's home. Nor could he risk going to the restaurant.

He didn't know a lot about the people who were behind these operations, but he knew enough to know that they were most likely keeping an eye on things. And Ty couldn't take that risk.

But Ty knew where guys Tommy's age liked to hang out on the island.

It didn't matter that the breeze was sharp today. Surfers around here like to get into the water whenever they could, especially when the waves were good.

He was able to catch Tommy on the beach before the teen went out surfing.

"What can I do for you?" Tommy paused beside his surfboard.

"I know that you've been making deliveries for the restaurant every night," Ty started.

The boy's face went slack. "What?"

"You don't have to pretend like you don't know what I'm talking about. I already have confirmation of it."

Tommy looked around. "That was supposed to be on the down low. He said if anybody else found out then he was going to stop ordering from us. I make thirty bucks a night from those deliveries. But I promised to be discreet."

"I know. And I don't want to get you in trouble. That's not why I'm here."

Tommy eyed him. "Then what do you want?"

"The people you're dealing with . . . they're dangerous. Very dangerous. I don't think you realize what you've gotten yourself in the middle of."

Tommy glanced around again. "They seem pretty normal."

"That's because they're also great actors. It's what makes them so good at what they do."

Tommy swallowed hard and gripped his surfboard. "So why are we talking right now?"

"I need to know the address for these deliveries."

"But…"

"Tommy, you can't be involved with these guys. When they're done with you, they won't think twice about getting rid of you to make sure that you continue to be discreet. Do you get my drift?"

Tommy's eyes widened. "Yeah, I get what you're saying."

"I need you to tell me the address where you've been going and anything of note that you've seen or heard when you made those deliveries. And tonight when you guys get the call to bring food we need to have somebody else take your place. You need to put as much distance between these people and yourself as possible."

"But…I could use the money."

Ty stepped closer. "These people are assassins for hire. You don't want to mess with them."

"They kill people?" Tommy swallowed hard and stared another moment before nodding his head rapidly. "Whatever you need. I'll do it."

"THIS IS where he said they're staying." Ty pointed to an area on the map.

Cassidy squinted, trying to get a better idea of where these people were located.

"It looks like he just pointed at the water," she said.

Ty nodded. "They're staying in a houseboat. Honestly, it's pretty smart of them. That's not one of the areas where we normally check."

"It's true," Mac added. "The people staying on those houseboats are from different families that come and go at various times of the year. The boats are mostly empty now. Plus they're far enough off the beaten path that we don't see them that often."

"So this whole time they have been staying on the island?" Cassidy shook her head, nearly wanting to kick herself. She'd assumed that at least one of them had left the island at some point.

But they'd both been here the whole time.

If she had been able to locate them earlier, they could have stopped a lot of this danger before it ever happened.

"These people know what they're doing." Ty locked his gaze with hers, almost as if reading her thoughts. "They know the best places to hide out. It's what they do."

"I understand." This wasn't a time for her to feel

sorry for herself or even to kick herself for any mistakes. This was the time to move forward.

"We need to make sure that they're surrounded, so that once we get there, they don't try to run," Ty said.

"Ordinarily, in a circumstance like this, I'd call in the Coast Guard," Cassidy started.

"How would you feel if we used the Blackout guys for this? They're still here for another week or so before they start a big job we have coming up. They could monitor the waterways. And they are familiar with shock and awe tactics. You could also get some of your guys involved too. With all of us involved, we could have them surrounded."

She shook her head. "The less people who know about this the better. I love the guys here on the force, but even the fact that they might know anything puts them in danger."

"I understand," Mac added. "But we still might need more manpower. We have the three of us here, and the four guys with Blackout. Plus, who's going to take Tommy's place?"

Cassidy leaned back. "I've been thinking about that. There's only one person who comes to mind who might work. Officer Banks. I know I just said I didn't want to involve any of my guys, but he's the only one who looks anything remotely like Tommy. If the guy sees somebody else coming, it's going to all be over."

"Do you think you can trust Banks?" Mac asked.

"He's never done anything to show me that I can't," Cassidy said. "Still, I hate to involve him. But I don't have any other good solutions."

"I think you should talk to him. He seems pretty loyal. See if we can get him on board."

Cassidy nodded and then looked at the time on her watch. "We are down to two hours now. We really need to get a feel of the landscape of that area before we get out there. We don't have a lot of time. But we have to make sure that these people don't see us."

"You're right," Mac said. "And the Shacklefords are sharp. They're not going to fall for any of the normal ruses, like pretending to be with the plumbing company. Anything we do will have to be in secret."

Cassidy nodded. "We better get busy."

She couldn't deny that a knot of nerves had formed in her stomach.

CHAPTER THIRTY-NINE

AN HOUR LATER, Ty and his guys had used a thermal camera to determine there were three people inside the houseboat. The vessel was located at the end of another long lane, not terribly far from where the body of Sandra Myers had been found.

Eight boat slips had been set up there to accommodate houseboats. The other boats were not currently occupied. A black car matching the description of the one that had almost run Cassidy and Bradshaw over had been hidden in the woods.

Two guys from Blackout had taken a boat out to monitor the waters in the distance. Meanwhile, Mac and Ty would act as an extra set of eyes and protection from the woods near the place.

As soon as Cassidy confirmed that these guys

were inside, she would step forward to confront them while her backup remained in waiting.

A lot could go wrong. She knew that.

But this was what she'd trained for. Still, she, Mac, and Ty were trying to work out all the details. As soon as Tommy got that call, they needed to be ready to jump into action.

As the three of them were discussing details, Cassidy's phone rang. She recognized the number. It was Hollick.

She answered and put him on speaker.

"Cassidy," he started. "Time is running out."

"I know. But you promised to give me two days."

"If I don't get back with this person soon, then he's going to destroy me. I can't let that happen." Panic laced his voice.

"I understand your concern. But I need those full two days. Just give me a little bit longer."

"I hope you're working on something."

Cassidy started to confirm that she was, but she thought better of it. She wasn't sure she could trust Hollick. The last thing she wanted was to spill information to him that might ruin this whole operation.

"I'm doing what I can," she finally said. "But I need the time you promised."

Cassidy held her breath, halfway fearing Hollick would rescind his offer.

She waited for his response, the moments ticking by as if in slow motion.

"Fine," Hollick finally said. "You have until the end of the day today. But no longer."

"Thank you." Her throat burned as she muttered the words.

Part of her didn't want to thank this man. Hollick was clearly only looking out for himself and his own political career. He gave hardly any thought to anybody else.

At least Cassidy knew that and didn't have to guess about his intentions. Still, she hated to thank a man she had no admiration for.

As soon as she ended the call, someone knocked at her door.

She looked up and saw Watkins standing there.

Quickly, she pulled a stack of files over the map she'd been looking at.

Watkins couldn't learn about what they were doing.

Especially not after what Stephens had told her.

WATKINS' eyes went to her desk. "Is everything okay?"

Cassidy nodded, maybe a little too quickly. "Everything is fine. Thank you."

He still eyed her a moment, then glanced at Ty and Mac. She quickly introduced them before turning back to Watkins.

"What brings you here?" she asked.

"I came to see if there are any updates on the case."

Cassidy swallowed hard. She prided herself on being honest. But this situation . . . it was different. "As you know, you asked me not to be a part of this case."

He narrowed his gaze. "I hear you. I just didn't know if you had heard anything that we didn't, since you have contacts in this area."

"We haven't gotten any tips or anything that might interest you." Cassidy's words were honest, but guilt still pressed on her. "Is there anything that you can share?"

She already knew the answer before he even opened his mouth.

"No, not yet."

She nodded slowly. "I hope you find the person who is responsible for this."

"Don't worry. We will. We already have almost twenty other agents here on the island. If these people who did this to Sandra are still here, we will find them."

"And I hope you put them away for life when you do."

He stared at her another moment before nodding. "I'll let you go back to your meeting."

He glanced at her desk one more time before offering a curt nod and leaving.

Maybe he suspected something, but at least he wasn't pushing the issue.

As soon as she saw Watkins step from the police station, she released her breath. That was close.

"He seems like a real peach," Mac said.

"It's too risky to share any of this information with him," Ty said.

"I agree," Mac said. "Besides, the more people who know about this, the higher probability that this will be ruined."

Cassidy nodded knowing their words were true.

Ty's phone rang and he answered. When the call ended, he announced, "These guys placed their dinner order early tonight. Unfortunately, we're not going to have time to do any more planning. We need to get moving. Now."

CHAPTER FORTY

CASSIDY TALKED to Banks and explained just enough about the situation to him to put him at ease. He agreed to help her and promised to keep the details quiet.

Several minutes later, Tommy met her and Banks at a restroom beside the pier.

The men exchanged clothing, and Tommy agreed to let them use his car for the delivery. They needed to do everything they could not to raise the Shacklefords' suspicions.

Cassidy glanced back and forth between the two men after they changed in the restroom. They definitely weren't twins, but, at first glance, they looked similar enough.

Ty and his guys were already in place near the

houseboat. Cassidy needed to take her place in the woods before Banks arrived.

"Give me a few minutes so I can get a head start," Cassidy instructed Banks.

"Will do." He climbed into Tommy's beat-up old red sedan and waited.

She took off and a few minutes later parked her SUV two streets over before slipping through the trees. She watched her steps as she moved through the forest, careful not to draw any attention to herself.

As the saying went, it was showtime. Everything was riding on what happened next.

The realization made her feel like she couldn't breathe, but she kept her cool.

Finally, Cassidy reached her designated spot. She stood behind a large tree, her gun drawn. She had to make sure the Shacklefords were inside before they made any drastic moves.

Everyone else—Ty, Mac, Colton, Dez, and Griff —were also in place. Cassidy drew in a deep breath and stared at the boat, waiting for the moment she sprang into action.

She and Ty would go in first. But, at their signal, the rest of the guys would step in.

The vessel wasn't incredibly large—maybe six

hundred square feet at the most. The outside was painted white, and there was a small deck up top. No furniture had been placed outside.

The boats around it were of varying sizes and shapes, but most looked as if they'd been untouched for a while. A small, gravel parking lot stood at the start of the area and a sandy path led to the bulkhead and boat slips.

Cassidy watched carefully as Banks pulled up to the houseboat in Tommy's car. As he climbed out and started forward, he gripped the paper bag full of food.

His body language looked relaxed enough—anyone who didn't know what was happening probably wouldn't be suspicious. Banks walked on the dock, onto the boat, and left the bag by the door just as directed.

These guys would never see his face up close.

But Cassidy had no doubt that they were watching.

Delivery made, Banks climbed back into Tommy's car and pulled away. When the vehicle disappeared down the road, the houseboat door opened.

Lars Shackleford glanced around, his beady eyes searching for any signs of trouble.

Then he reached down and snatched the bag before quickly retreating inside.

It was him.

The Shacklefords were definitely here on this island.

And now it was time for Cassidy and the rest of the crew to act.

Shock and awe, she reminded herself. Shock and awe.

CASSIDY MOTIONED TO TY.

They needed to move. Now.

Quietly, they made their way to the houseboat. Cassidy and Ty flanked either side of the front door.

When Cassidy gave a nod, Ty kicked the door open, and they flooded inside the place.

"Police!" Cassidy announced.

The Shacklefords stood at attention with their guns drawn.

Somehow, these guys had been expecting them.

Lars looked as arrogant as ever in his all-black outfit. His blond hair was cut short and spiked atop his head. His icy blue eyes and pale skin almost made him look frostier than ever.

"Put your guns down or we'll shoot her," Lars said.

Cassidy glanced over and saw Emma Shackleford pointing her gun at Alexandria, who was tied to a wooden chair near a small desk.

Alexandria looked terrified.

One of her eyes was black. Her hair was disheveled. Her lip busted.

Maybe Alexandria *wasn't* working for them—at least, not of her own accord.

A knot formed in Cassidy's gut. "You're not going to shoot Alexandria. She's too valuable to you."

"Nobody is valuable to us," Emma hissed. Like her husband, she was dressed in all black. Her dark hair had been pulled back in a bun, and she'd donned red lipstick. "My husband said put your guns down. Do it. Now."

Cassidy weighed her options before saying, "That's not going to happen."

"Aren't the FBI supposed to be the ones who arrest us?" Lars' eyes gleamed with satisfaction. He didn't try to hide the fact that he might have inside information. "This isn't your case, is it, Chief?"

This guy was trying to get under Cassidy's skin—and it was starting to work. She had to nip that in the bud.

"I said put your guns down." Cassidy stared at them, still gripping her gun.

"Don't think I won't shoot her." Lars jammed his gun into Alexandria's chest until she whimpered.

The woman had tears streaming down her cheeks and a look of desperation in her eyes.

Ty and Cassidy glanced at each other again, silently communicating.

Finally, they both lowered their weapons, knowing that Lars would act. Emma reached forward and grabbed the guns, placing them on a table behind her.

Cassidy couldn't allow an innocent civilian to get hurt. Lars had known that.

She was going to let these two think they were in control. But ultimately, they couldn't be. Not if Cassidy wanted to win this.

She lifted a prayer, praying for the best right now.

CHAPTER FORTY-ONE

CASSIDY RAISED HER HANDS HIGHER. "There's no need for you to hurt Alexandria."

"You're not the one calling the shots here." Lars barked. "I knew you were out there—we have hidden security cameras. However, it appears I underestimated you two."

"You think you're smarter than everybody else," Cassidy said. "There's a certain danger in that."

Lars' eyes gleamed again. "I *know* I'm smarter than everyone else! But you two showing up here means I have more collateral damage to clean up."

Cassidy swallowed hard. She didn't like the sound of that. "You do know we have a crew waiting outside. Even if you kill us, you're still going to have to deal with them. Not to mention the FBI. What exactly is your plan of action now?"

Lars shrugged. The man seemed unfazed, but his lips twitched again, curling down slightly. "I'll figure it out."

"But will you? Because I feel like you've been feeling your way through this entire thing."

"We haven't been feeling our way through anything!" Lars said. "You don't know what you're talking about."

Cassidy was getting under their skin. If she wasn't careful, that could backfire. But if she played her cards just right . . .

In the meantime, she wanted more answers.

"I know the CIA fired you. Accused you of killing one of your colleagues. You were going to go to jail for a long time, and that was a shame. You were two of the best agents out there, or so I've heard."

"We didn't kill Hank!" Emma said. "We were set up. There was no way we were taking the fall for what someone else did."

"So why become killers?" Her timing might be bad, but Cassidy truly did want to know.

"Anger." Lars nearly spat out the words. "Why play by the rules when the rules get you nowhere?"

"But you had to have a purpose," Cassidy continued. "You don't do things without a reason."

"Because we know who framed us," Emma said, her voice just above a simmer. "And, as soon as we have enough money, we're going to show the world what kind of person he really is."

"Who?" Ty asked. "Who framed you?"

"Gerald Mecklenburg—our former boss. He found out that Hank had discovered some backroom deals he was working. In order to silence Hank, he ended his life."

"How do you know that?" Cassidy asked.

"Because Hank told us what he knew," Lars said. "The next day, he was dead."

"But I don't understand," Cassidy said. "Why hurt these innocent people? How does that fit with your agenda?"

"Most of the people we've hurt haven't been all that innocent. They've been criminals—the white-collar sort who don't think they'll ever get caught."

Cassidy glanced at Alexandria and saw her eyes were still wide and frightened. She had to figure a way to get the woman out of here safely.

She glanced back at Lars. "Why did you take the job with the Manchester family then? How does that fit?"

"You haven't figured it out?" Satisfaction gleamed in Lars' gaze.

"Because you wanted to take down Hollick." The details clicked in place in Cassidy's mind. "In the process, you discovered Alexandria used to be a hacker. Not only that, she was pretty good at it. So you decided to use that to your advantage. You picked key people and decided to look for any type of secret in their background."

"And that's when we discovered your real identity." Lars grinned. "Wasn't that convenient?"

Cassidy ignored him. "Then you started asking for money. You made a little game out of it."

"Of course, we had to research you," Emma growled. "Not only your cases back in Seattle, but everything you've done since you've come here. Some people still think you're a superhero, almost like that silly cartoon someone made of you calling you Commotio Cordis."

Commotio Cordis was the name some on the fringes had given her after she'd taken down DH-7's leader. Some had even created cartoons and anime featuring her.

Cassidy hadn't heard that name in a long time. "I'm not the superhero. But I am persistent."

"Well, that persistence could get you killed." Lars raised his gun again.

Cassidy felt her throat tightening but tried not to show it. "You figured if you could find enough people to hold things over that you could eventually get money."

"I'm tired of talking about it," Lars said. "You're only trying to distract me."

"Distract you from what? I don't even have a weapon. You took it."

The smirk reappeared across Lars' face. "Yes, I did, didn't I? Now I need to consider my options. I can't leave here with both of you. If I turn my back on you, you'll both try to attack. So that's not going to work. In fact, I can't think of any way to make a run for it with both of you alive. The best thing I can do is take you all as hostages, get out of here, and then kill you."

Cassidy's throat tightened even more.

"Why don't you slow down here?" Ty said. "Let's talk this out."

"Navy SEALs aren't exactly known for talking things out, are they?" Lars snorted. "We know all about you two. In fact, we couldn't decide which of you we really wanted to target the most. Fortunately for you, your wife wins. Maybe if something happens to her, you can live a halfway normal life here in Lantern Beach."

"You used to work for the government," Cassidy said. "You tried to do what was right. I don't understand how you turned from American heroes into who you are now."

"Gerald Mecklenburg betrayed us." Emma said the words through clenched teeth. "We'll never forgive him for that."

"People need to pay," Lars said. "People who use their power to get what they want. We pulled you into this because we needed to keep you running in circles so you wouldn't find us. Apparently, that didn't work."

More questions begged for Cassidy's attention. "What about the window guy? Rob? He's the one who doesn't make sense to me."

"He's Mecklenburg's best friend," Emma said. "We're going to use him to get to Mecklenburg. But first, we knew we could use him here."

"And Sandra Myers?" Ty asked.

"She was dirty." Lars sneered as he said the words. "She was Mecklenburg's right-hand woman until she got transferred to the FBI. We told her if she didn't come that we'd kill her mother, who happened to be in a nursing home. We arranged for her mom to be transferred to a new facility without Sandra's knowledge. We needed to keep her on her toes."

"What was the point of bringing her here, though?" Cassidy asked.

"To kill her, of course. Then to set it up so you'd think it was Alexandria."

Cassidy's blood seemed to freeze in her veins. These people truly were heartless.

"More games?" Cassidy shook her head. "You love playing those, don't you?"

"As a matter of fact, I do." Lars raised his gun. "Now, no more talking! Now, this is what I'm going to do. I'm going to tell everybody that you're a dead woman unless they let us get away. Are you ready for some fun?"

TY DIDN'T like the way any of this was going. Thankfully, they hadn't come here without a backup plan. Though they hadn't had time to talk everything through, Ty had been in enough life-or-death situations to know never to go in without backup.

But even backup could be risky, and Ty had to choose just the right moment before he acted.

He had no doubt that these people truly would take him and Cassidy hostage.

And he didn't know what would happen after that.

Before they hurt Cassidy, they were going to have to get through him. Ty would do whatever it took to protect her. It had always been that way, and it always would be.

"Why don't you let the ladies go and keep me?" Ty stepped closer. "You really only need one hostage."

"If that's the case, then we will just keep Alexandria," Lars said. "She's proven to be very useful."

Cassidy turned to Alexandria, defiance in her gaze. "Annabeth has been staying with us. Your daughter is safe, and she's doing great."

A small cry escaped from Alexandria, as if relief had rushed through her. "Thank you. Thank you! I've been so worried."

"I know they probably threatened that if you didn't do their dirty work, they would hurt her," Cassidy continued. "But we haven't let anybody get close."

"I just want my family back," Alexandria said.

"We don't want anyone to get hurt here either," Ty said.

"I know what you're doing!" Lars yelled, his face reddening. "You're buying time. And now I'm tired. I'm *really* tired of this. We don't have any more time to waste."

Lars stepped toward Cassidy.

Ty knew he had to act.

He dropped the flash bang down from his sleeve where he'd kept it tucked. The next instant, he tossed the device across the room.

A bang sounded, sending everyone scrambling for cover.

They had to get this right . . . or they would all be goners.

CHAPTER FORTY-TWO

CASSIDY WATCHED as Ty lunged toward Lars. The two men collided.

He would take care of Lars. Meanwhile, Cassidy needed to subdue Emma.

The woman sprang toward Cassidy and threw her on the floor.

Emma smashed Cassidy's hands against the floor and pinned her down.

"You're not going to get away with this." The woman's nostrils flared as she glared down at Cassidy.

"Watch me."

In one motion, Cassidy pushed the woman off her and flipped places with her. Now, Cassidy hovered over the woman, pressing down on Emma's arms and legs so she couldn't move.

"You think you're so smart," Emma said through clenched teeth. "We'll see about that."

Emma used all of her strength to push Cassidy off.

Cassidy landed on her side. As she saw Emma start toward her again, Cassidy's eyes went to the gun on the table.

If she could just reach it.

Beside her, Ty let out a grunt.

Cassidy's gaze slipped toward him. She needed to see what was going on. Needed to know that Ty was okay.

But the sound distracted her enough that Emma wrapped her arms around Cassidy's throat, cutting off her airway. Cassidy gasped for breath as she tried to fight the woman off.

Using her body as leverage, Cassidy pivoted and sent Emma flying over her shoulder. The woman landed on the table, and the wood cracked.

Alexandria, still bound around the chair, scooted back.

Just then, Blackout agents rushed inside, guns raised.

"Stop or we'll shoot!" Colton yelled.

Lars and Emma seemed to freeze as they realized they were surrounded.

Cassidy quickly grabbed her own gun and pointed it at Emma. As she did, Griff handcuffed the woman.

"It's over," Cassidy said. "You guys won't be hurting anyone again any time soon."

As Ty handcuffed Lars, the man smirked at Cassidy. "I thought you should know, I just sent out a text message. Now the world knows who you really are."

AS SOON AS TY HEARD LARS' words, panic washed over him.

Had the man really sent out that message?

Ty would deal with that in a moment.

Right now, they needed to take these guys into custody.

As his Blackout agents ushered the Shacklefords from the boat, Cassidy rushed toward Alexandria and untied her. "Are you okay?"

The woman nodded. As soon as her binds were loosened, Alexandria threw her arms around Cassidy and began sobbing. "Thank you. Thank you for everything. I'm so sorry that I had to uncover what I did. I didn't want to. But they forced me."

"I know. It's going to be okay."

"Can I see my daughter? And how about Joe? Where is he? They told me he died."

"He didn't die," Ty said. "He's in the hospital in a coma."

Alexandria let out a cry, her eyes a mix of joy and sorrow. "At least there's hope."

"There's always hope," Cassidy said. "Always."

The two of them stepped from the houseboat.

Just as they did, five cars sped onto the scene.

The FBI.

They were here.

And now Cassidy was going to have some explaining to do.

Ty prayed that it worked out for the best.

But the good news was that now the Shacklefords would be behind bars. Their shenanigans couldn't hurt anybody else again.

But there was some damage that had already been done. Plus, there could be a dirty FBI agent in their midst. Their trouble wasn't over yet . . . but at least maybe they'd have a moment to breathe.

CHAPTER FORTY-THREE

"WHAT DO you think you're doing?" Watkins stormed toward Cassidy once she was standing on the sandy path with Alexandria.

"We were following up on a lead." Cassidy raised her chin, determined to stay strong.

"I thought we agreed to keep each other in the loop." He stopped in front of her and scowled.

"I couldn't be sure this tip had anything to do with the case you're investigating. Turned out, it did." Cassidy shrugged. "Here I thought someone was just doing drugs inside . . ."

Watkins glanced around and shook his head. "It looks like you have plenty of your other guys here on hand just in case."

"One can never be too careful."

Watkins leaned closer and lowered his voice. "What exactly are you thinking, Cassidy Chambers? You know the FBI took over this case."

"How about a thank you for both recovering a victim and for arresting two of the most wanted criminals in the United States?"

"It doesn't change the fact that you went against orders," Watkins said. "What if it hadn't turned out this way? What if someone had died?"

"Then I would have had to live with that decision every day for the rest of my life. Believe me, I thought about that." The truth saturated Cassidy's words.

A paramedic arrived and led Alexandria away to be checked out.

Watkins continued to glare at her. "I don't know why you didn't tell me that this was going down."

Cassidy swallowed hard as she remembered Stephens' words. "It's like I said. I didn't *know* what was going on. By the time I realized that these guys were actually here, it was too late."

Watkins' grunt showed that he didn't believe her. "We'll be taking over from here. You should just be thankful I'm not charging you with obstruction of justice."

"What are you going to do with Alexandria?"

Cassidy held her breath as she waited for the answer.

"She's not innocent in all of this."

"Whatever she did, she did it under coercion."

"That may be true. That doesn't mean that there won't be any consequences for her actions."

Alexandria let out a cry in the distance as she sat on a gurney. She'd obviously heard what he'd said.

"Please." Alexandria rose and stepped toward Cassidy until a paramedic urged her back down. "Take care of Annabeth for me until I can get back to her. Please."

Cassidy nodded, sorrow gripping her heart. "Of course. Whatever you need."

Cassidy glanced back at Watkins.

But maybe this was all over.

Except for one thing.

Lars said that he had broadcast Cassidy's real identity to the world.

Cassidy didn't know exactly what that meant . . . but it couldn't be good.

"YOU DID THE RIGHT THING," Mac said.

Everybody still lingered on the scene, and they

would be here for quite a while. There was a lot of evidence to comb through, all of which Cassidy had been instructed to keep her nose out of.

She hadn't been asked to leave the crime scene yet, so she hadn't.

"I'm not really sure what the right thing was in this situation," Cassidy said.

"It's like you told Special Agent Watkins. Two criminals have been arrested, Alexandria has been rescued, and she's in one piece. I'd say that was a win."

"Mac . . ." Cassidy lowered her voice. "Before Lars was arrested, he said he sent out a broadcast about who I really was."

Mac shrugged as if she'd just told him forecasters were calling for rain later. "I wouldn't worry about that."

"How can I not worry?" Of all people, Cassidy had thought Mac would be able to see the complexity of the situation.

He raised something from inside his pocket. "I thought they might try to pull something like that. So I pressed this."

Cassidy leaned closer and stared at the device in his hands. "Is that a . . . cell phone jammer?"

Mac grinned. "You didn't hear it from me."

"Mac . . . did you really?"

"For you? I sure did."

The breath left her lungs. "Thank you. You're a real lifesaver."

"I can't let anybody find out who my favorite police chief really is. Then we might lose you here in Lantern Beach, and I can't let that happen." Emotion —and loyalty—glimmered in his gaze.

Ty appeared behind Cassidy and placed his hand on her lower back. "It looks like someone's doing some celebrating over here."

Cassidy turned to him. "I'll tell you all about it in a minute. But it's good news."

"I'm glad. Because I could use some good news."

"I think we all could." Cassidy was ready to put all this behind her.

But one other thing bothered her—all that information the Shacklefords had on people . . . it was somewhere on these people's devices. If the FBI found it . . . would that mean Cassidy was still in danger?

CHAPTER FORTY-FOUR

CASSIDY SLAPPED her hand over the pile of cards in a winning move before offering a triumphant smile. "Who's the official UNO champion now?"

Cassidy would think with all the games being played around her lately that a simple card game wouldn't have any appeal. But every time Cassidy saw Annabeth smile, she wanted to do whatever it took to keep that grin on the girl's face.

"Cassidy has won the past two games." Ty lowered his voice as he looked at her. "You have no mercy, do you?"

"Hey, I won fair and square," Cassidy said. "What more can I say? Sometimes, the hand you're dealt is a good one, and sometimes it's not. That's what it all boils down to."

That statement was so applicable, not only to Uno but to life in general, wasn't it?

Cassidy and Ty exchanged a smile before Ty asked, "Who wants to play another round?"

Annabeth raised her hand in the air.

Cassidy smiled again, enjoying the simple moment at the house with Ty and Annabeth.

The good news was that since Alexandria had been found, the legal guardianship case presented by the attorneys had been dropped. Pender had no legal precedent to take over the Manchesters' affairs, thank goodness. In fact, those two lawyers had been targets of the Shacklefords also. Cassidy didn't know what the two had on the attorneys or what they wanted from them, but it was enough that Pender had forged a lot of that paperwork.

In another strange twist, the Shacklefords' cell phones were missing and their computer had been wiped. Watkins had asked Cassidy about it several times, but she hadn't taken the phones. Lars had his right before he'd been arrested.

So what had happened to the phones? And what kind of information had been on that computer?

Watkins hadn't been happy with Cassidy, but he'd let her go with a warning.

Still, Cassidy worried about how many people

might know the truth. The more people who knew, the more her life was in danger. And, by default, the more endangered the lives were of those around her as well.

When someone knocked at the door, Cassidy rose. She knew who was here. She'd been waiting for them to arrive.

She offered a tight but hopefully reassuring smile to Annabeth as she paused. Then, taking a deep breath, Cassidy started to the door and opened it.

Special Agent Watkins stood there. As usual, he wore a scowl and his lips were pulled in a permanent frown.

"Chief," he muttered.

"Agent," she responded with an equal lack of enthusiasm.

It was the woman who was beside Watkins who got Cassidy's attention.

Alexandria Manchester.

She was being held until the FBI could figure out exactly what her involvement was in this mess. Cassidy felt certain the woman would be released, but they had to go through due process first.

"Are you ready for this?" Cassidy asked Alexandria.

Maybe Cassidy should be asking herself that same question.

Alexandria nodded and wiped her palms on the sides of her jeans. She looked nervous also. But at least all the signs of her captivity were gone. No longer could Cassidy see the bruises on her face or the burns around her wrists.

The next instant, Cassidy turned and saw Annabeth standing there.

"Mom!" the girl whispered, her voice hoarse.

Annabeth ran into her mother's arms.

Tears filled Cassidy's eyes as she watched them. Ty stood beside Cassidy and wrapped an arm around her waist as they witnessed the reunion.

It really was beautiful, just as Cassidy had expected it would be. But a surprising sadness filled her as well. She knew her time with Annabeth was probably coming to an end soon.

Cassidy knew that was the way it should be. But she'd miss the girl and knew that the house would feel empty without her.

"How's the case going?" Cassidy asked Watkins as he strode up beside her.

It had been three days since they had spoken.

"We're uncovering more and more all the time."

Watkins regarded her with that cold, unreadable look again.

"I can imagine."

"There are still some missing pieces that we're trying to find. But we will."

Cassidy nodded. "I'm sure you will."

But her throat tightened as she said the words.

Even though big pieces of the puzzle had been resolved, Cassidy couldn't help but think there were enough dangling threads out there still that this wasn't quite over. What else had the Shacklefords set in motion?

She didn't know, and she really didn't even want to find out.

But for now, she would take a minute to breathe . . . and stand in awe of what they'd accomplished so far.

~~~

Thank you so much for reading *Shock and Awe*. If you enjoyed this book, please consider leaving a review.
~~~

Order your copy HERE.

LANTERN BEACH MYSTERIES

Hidden Currents

You can take the detective out of the investigation, but you can't take the investigator out of the detective. A notorious gang puts a bounty on Detective Cady Matthews's head after she takes down their leader, leaving her no choice but to hide until she can testify at trial. But her temporary home across the country on a remote North Carolina island isn't as peaceful as she initially thinks. Living under the new identity of Cassidy Livingston, she struggles to keep her investigative skills tucked away, especially after a body washes ashore. When local police bungle the murder investigation, she can't resist stepping in. But

Cassidy is supposed to be keeping a low profile. One wrong move could lead to both her discovery and her demise. Can she bring justice to the island . . . or will the hidden currents surrounding her pull her under for good?

Flood Watch

The tide is high, and so is the danger on Lantern Beach. Still in hiding after infiltrating a dangerous gang, Cassidy Livingston just has to make it a few more months before she can testify at trial and resume her old life. But trouble keeps finding her, and Cassidy is pulled into a local investigation after a man mysteriously disappears from the island she now calls home. A recurring nightmare from her time undercover only muddies things, as does a visit from the parents of her handsome ex-Navy SEAL neighbor. When a friend's life is threatened, Cassidy must make choices that put her on the verge of blowing her cover. With a flood watch on her emotions and her life in a tangle, will Cassidy find the truth? Or will her past finally drown her?

Storm Surge

A storm is brewing hundreds of miles away, but its effects are devastating even from afar. Laid-back, loose, and light: that's Cassidy Livingston's new motto. But when a makeshift boat with a bloody cloth inside washes ashore near her oceanfront home, her detective instincts shift into gear . . . again. Seeking clues isn't the only thing on her mind—romance is heating up with next-door neighbor and former Navy SEAL Ty Chambers as well. Her heart wants the love and stability she's longed for her entire life. But her hidden identity only leads to a tidal wave of turbulence. As more answers emerge about the boat, the danger around her rises, creating a treacherous swell that threatens to reveal her past. Can Cassidy mind her own business, or will the storm surge of violence and corruption that has washed ashore on Lantern Beach leave her life in wreckage?

Dangerous Waters

Danger lurks on the horizon, leaving only two choices: find shelter or flee. Cassidy Livingston's new identity has begun to feel as comfortable as her favorite sweater. She's been tucked away on Lantern Beach for weeks, waiting to testify against a deadly gang, and is settling in to a new life she wants to last forever. When she thinks she spots someone malevolent from her past, panic swells inside her. If an enemy has found her, Cassidy won't be the only one who's a target. Everyone she's come to love will also be at risk. Dangerous waters threaten to pull her into an overpowering chasm she may never escape. Can Cassidy survive what lies ahead? Or has the tide fatally turned against her?

Perilous Riptide

Just when the current seems safer, an unseen danger emerges and threatens to destroy everything. When Cassidy Livingston finds a journal hidden deep in the recesses of her ice cream truck, her curiosity kicks into high gear. Islanders suspect that Elsa, the journal's owner, didn't die accidentally. Her final entry indicates their suspicions might be correct and that what Elsa observed on her final night may have led to her demise. Against the advice of Ty Chambers, her former Navy SEAL boyfriend, Cassidy taps into her detective skills and hunts for answers. But her search only leads to a skeletal body and trouble for both of them. As helplessness threatens to drown her, Cassidy is desperate to turn back time. Can Cassidy find what she needs to navigate the perilous situation? Or will the riptide surrounding her threaten everyone and everything Cassidy loves?

Deadly Undertow

The current's fatal pull is powerful, but so is one detective's will to live. When someone from Cassidy Livingston's past shows up on Lantern Beach and warns her of impending peril, opposing currents collide, threatening to drag her under. Running would be easy. But leaving would break her heart. Cassidy must decipher between the truth and lies, between reality and deception. Even more importantly, she must decide whom to trust and whom to fear. Her life depends on it. As danger rises and answers surface, everything Cassidy thought she knew is tested. In order to survive, Cassidy must take drastic measures and end the battle against the ruthless gang DH-7 once and for all. But if her final mission fails, the consequences will be as deadly as the raging undertow.

LANTERN BEACH ROMANTIC SUSPENSE

Tides of Deception

Change has come to Lantern Beach: a new police chief, a new season, and . . . a new romance? Austin Brooks has loved Skye Lavinia from the moment they met, but the walls she keeps around her seem impenetrable. Skye knows Austin is the best thing to ever happen to her. Yet she also knows that if he learns the truth about her past, he'd be a fool not to run. A chance encounter brings secrets bubbling to the surface, and danger soon follows. Are the life-threatening events plaguing them really accidents . . . or is someone trying to send a deadly message? With the tides on Lantern Beach come deception and lies. One question remains—who will be swept away as the water shifts? And will it bring the end for Austin and Skye, or merely the beginning?

Shadow of Intrigue

For her entire life, Lisa Garth has felt like a supporting character in the drama of life. The designation never bothered her—until now. Lantern Beach, where she's settled and runs a popular restaurant, has boarded up for the season. The slower pace leaves her with too much time alone. Braden Dillinger came to Lantern Beach to try to heal. The former Special Forces officer returned from battle with invisible scars and diminished hope. But his recovery is hampered by the fact that an unknown enemy is trying to kill him. From the moment Lisa and Braden meet, danger ignites around them, and both are drawn into a web of intrigue that turns their lives upside down. As shadows creep in, will Lisa and Braden be able to shine a light on the peril around them? Or will the encroaching darkness turn their worst nightmares into reality?

Storm of Doubt

A pastor who's lost faith in God. A romance writer who's lost faith in love. A faceless man with a deadly obsession. Nothing has felt right in Pastor Jack Wilson's world since his wife died two years ago. He hoped coming to Lantern Beach might help soothe the ragged edges of his soul. Instead, he feels more alone than ever. Novelist Juliette Grace came to the island to hide away. Though her professional life has never been better, her personal life has imploded. Her husband left her and a stalker's threats have grown more and more dangerous. When Jack saves Juliette from an attack, he sees the terror in her gaze and knows he must protect her. But when danger strikes again, will Jack be able to keep her safe? Or will the approaching storm prove too strong to withstand?

Winds of Danger

Wes O'Neill is perfectly content to hang with his friends and enjoy island life on Lantern Beach.

Something begins to change inside him when Paige Henderson sweeps into his life. But the beautiful newcomer is hiding painful secrets beneath her cheerful facade. Police dispatcher Paige Henderson came to Lantern Beach riddled with guilt and uncertainties after the fallout of a bad relationship. When she meets Wes, she begins to open up to the possibility of love again. But there's something Wes isn't telling her—something that could change everything. As the winds shift, doubts seep into Paige's mind. Can Paige and Wes trust each other, even as the currents work against them? Or is trouble from the past too much to overcome?

Rains of Remorse

A stranger invades her home, leaving Rebecca Jarvis terrified. Above all, she must protect the baby growing inside her. Since her estranged husband died suspiciously six months earlier, Rebecca has been determined to depend on no one but herself. Her chivalrous new neighbor appears to be an answer to prayer. But who is Levi Stoneman really? Rebecca wants to believe he can help her, but she can't ignore her instincts. As danger closes in, both Rebecca and Levi must figure out whom they can trust. With Rebecca's baby coming soon, there's no time to waste. Can the truth prevail . . . or will remorse overpower the best of intentions?

Torrents of Fear

The woman lingering in the crowd can't be Allison . . . can she? Because Allison was pronounced dead six years ago. Musician Carter Denver knows only one person who's capable of helping him find answers: Sadie Thompson, his estranged best friend and someone who also knew Allison. He needs to know if he's losing his mind or if Allison could have survived her car accident. Could Allison really be alive? If so, why is she trying to harm Carter and Sadie? As the two try to find answers, can Sadie keep her feelings for Carter hidden? Could he ever care for her, or is the man of her dreams still in love with the woman now causing his nightmares?

LANTERN BEACH PD

On the Lookout

When Cassidy Chambers accepted the job as police chief on Lantern Beach, she knew the island had its secrets. But a suspicious death with potentially far-reaching implications will test all her skills

—and threaten to reveal her true identity. Cassidy enlists the help of her husband, former Navy SEAL Ty Chambers. As they dig for answers, both uncover parts of their pasts that are best left buried. Not everything is as it seems, and they must figure out if their John Doe is connected to the secretive group that has moved onto the island. As facts materialize, danger on the island grows. Can Cassidy and Ty discover the truth about the shadowy crimes in their cozy community? Or has darkness permanently invaded their beloved Lantern Beach?

Attempt to Locate

A fun girls' night out turns into a nightmare when armed robbers barge into the store where Cassidy and her friends are shopping. As the situation escalates and the men escape, a massive manhunt launches on Lantern Beach to apprehend the dangerous trio. In the midst of the chaos, a potential foe asks for Cassidy's help. He needs to find his sister who fled from the secretive Gilead's Cove community on the island. But the more Cassidy learns about the seemingly untouchable group, the more her unease grows. The pressure to solve both cases continues to mount. But as the gravity of the situation rises, so does the danger. Cassidy is determined to protect the island and break up the cult . . . but doing so might cost her everything.

First Degree Murder

Police Chief Cassidy Chambers longs for a break from the recent crimes plaguing Lantern Beach. She simply wants to enjoy her friends' upcoming wedding, to prepare for the busy tourist season about to slam the island, and to gather all the dirt she can on the suspicious community that's invaded the town. But trouble explodes on the island, sending residents—including Cassidy—into a squall of uneasiness. Cassidy may have more than one enemy plotting her demise, and the collateral damage seems unthinkable. As the temperature rises, so does the pressure to find answers. Someone is determined that Lantern Beach would be better off without their new police chief. And for Cassidy, one wrong move could mean certain death.

Dead on Arrival

With a highly charged local election consuming the community, Police Chief Cassidy Chambers braces herself for a challenging day of breaking up petty conflicts and tamping down high emotions. But when widespread food poisoning spreads among potential voters across the island, Cassidy smells something rotten in the air. As Cassidy examines every possibility to uncover what's going on, local enigma Anthony Gilead again comes on her radar. The man is running for mayor and his cult-like following is growing at an alarming rate. Cassidy feels certain he has a spy embedded in her inner circle. The problem is that her pool of suspects gets deeper every day. Can Cassidy get to the bottom of what's eating away at her peaceful island home? Will voters turn out despite the outbreak of illness plaguing their tranquil town? And the even bigger question: Has darkness come to stay on Lantern Beach?

Plan of Action

A missing Navy SEAL. Danger at the boiling point. The ultimate showdown. When Police Chief Cassidy Chambers' husband, Ty, disappears, her world is turned upside down. His truck is discovered with blood inside, crashed in a ditch on Lantern Beach, but he's nowhere to be found. As they launch a manhunt to find him, Cassidy discovers that someone on the island has a deadly obsession with Ty. Meanwhile, Gilead's Cove seems to be imploding. As danger heightens, federal law enforcement officials are called in. The cult's growing threat could lead to the pinnacle standoff of good versus evil. A clear plan of action is needed or the results will be devastating. Will Cassidy find Ty in time, or will she face a gut-wrenching loss? Will Anthony Gilead finally be unmasked for who he really is and be brought to justice? Hundreds of innocent lives are at stake . . . and not everyone will come out alive.

LANTERN BEACH BLACKOUT

Dark Water

Colton Locke can't forget the black op that went terribly wrong. Desperate for a new start, he moves to Lantern Beach, North Carolina, and forms Blackout, a private security firm. Despite his hero status, he can't erase the mistakes he's made. For the past year, Elise Oliver hasn't been able to shake the feeling that there's more to her husband's death than she was told. When she finds a hidden box of his personal possessions, more questions—and suspicions—arise. The only person she trusts to help her is her husband's best friend, Colton Locke. Someone wants Elise dead. Is it because she knows too much? Or is it to keep her from finding the truth? The Blackout team must uncover dark secrets hiding beneath seemingly still waters. But those very secrets might just tear the team apart.

Safe Harbor

Guilt over past mistakes haunts former Navy SEAL Dez Rodriguez. When he's asked to guard a pop star during a music festival on Lantern Beach, he's all set for what he hopes is a breezy assignment. Bree hasn't found fame to be nearly as fulfilling as she dreamed. Instead, she's more like a carefully crafted character living out a pre-scripted story. When a stalker's threats become deadly, her life—and career—are turned upside down. From the start, Bree sees her temporary bodyguard as a player, and Dez sees Bree as a spoiled rich girl. But when they're thrown together in a fight for survival, both must learn to trust. Can Dez protect Bree—and his carefully guarded heart? Or will their safe harbor ultimately become their death trap?

Ripple Effect

Griff McIntyre never expected his ex-wife and three-year-old daughter to come to Lantern Beach. After an abduction attempt, they're desperate for safety. Now Griff's not letting either of them out of his sight. Bethany knows Griff is the only one who can protect them, despite the fact that he broke her heart. But she'll do anything to keep her daughter safe—even if it means playing nicely with a man she can't stand. As peril ripples through their lives, Griff and Bethany must work together to protect their daughter. But an unseen enemy wants something from them . . . and will stop at nothing to get it. When disaster strikes, can Griff keep his family safe? Or will past mistakes bring the ultimate failure?

Rising Tide

Benjamin James knows there's a traitor within his former command. The rest of his team might even think it's him. As danger closes in, he must clear himself and stop a deadly plot by a dangerous terrorist group. All CJ Compton wanted was a new start after her career ended under suspicion. Working as the house manager for private security group Blackout seems perfect. But there's more trouble here than what she left behind. As the tide rushes in, the stakes continue to rise. If the Blackout team fails, it's not just Lantern Beach at stake—it's the whole country. Can Benjamin and CJ overcome their differences and work together to find the truth?

COMPLETE BOOK LIST

Squeaky Clean Mysteries:

#1 Hazardous Duty

#2 Suspicious Minds

#2.5 It Came Upon a Midnight Crime (novella)

#3 Organized Grime

#4 Dirty Deeds

#5 The Scum of All Fears

#6 To Love, Honor and Perish

#7 Mucky Streak

#8 Foul Play

#9 Broom & Gloom

#10 Dust and Obey

#11 Thrill Squeaker

#11.5 Swept Away (novella)

#12 Cunning Attractions

#13 Cold Case: Clean Getaway

#14 Cold Case: Clean Sweep

#15 Cold Case: Clean Break

#16 Cleans to an End

While You Were Sweeping, A Riley Thomas Spinoff

The Sierra Files:

#1 Pounced

#2 Hunted

#3 Pranced

#4 Rattled

The Gabby St. Claire Diaries (a Tween Mystery series):

The Curtain Call Caper

The Disappearing Dog Dilemma

The Bungled Bike Burglaries

The Worst Detective Ever

#1 Ready to Fumble

#2 Reign of Error

#3 Safety in Blunders

#4 Join the Flub

#5 Blooper Freak

#6 Flaw Abiding Citizen

#7 Gaffe Out Loud

#8 Joke and Dagger

#9 Wreck the Halls

#10 Glitch and Famous

Raven Remington

Relentless 1

Relentless 2 (coming soon)

Holly Anna Paladin Mysteries:

#1 Random Acts of Murder

#2 Random Acts of Deceit

#2.5 Random Acts of Scrooge

#3 Random Acts of Malice

#4 Random Acts of Greed

#5 Random Acts of Fraud

#6 Random Acts of Outrage

#7 Random Acts of Iniquity

Lantern Beach Mysteries

#1 Hidden Currents

#2 Flood Watch

#3 Storm Surge

#4 Dangerous Waters

#5 Perilous Riptide

#6 Deadly Undertow

Lantern Beach Romantic Suspense

Tides of Deception

Shadow of Intrigue

Storm of Doubt

Winds of Danger

Rains of Remorse

Torrents of Fear

Lantern Beach P.D.

On the Lookout

Attempt to Locate

First Degree Murder

Dead on Arrival

Plan of Action

Lantern Beach Escape

Afterglow (a novelette)

Lantern Beach Blackout

Dark Water

Safe Harbor

Ripple Effect

Rising Tide

Crime á la Mode

Deadman's Float

Milkshake Up

Bomb Pop Threat

Banana Split Personalities

The Sidekick's Survival Guide

The Art of Eavesdropping

The Perks of Meddling

The Exercise of Interfering

The Practice of Prying

The Skill of Snooping

The Craft of Being Covert

Saltwater Cowboys

Saltwater Cowboy

Breakwater Protector

Cape Corral Keeper

Seagrass Secrets

Driftwood Danger

Carolina Moon Series

Home Before Dark

Gone By Dark

Wait Until Dark

Light the Dark

Taken By Dark

Suburban Sleuth Mysteries:
Death of the Couch Potato's Wife

Fog Lake Suspense:
Edge of Peril
Margin of Error
Brink of Danger
Line of Duty

Cape Thomas Series:
Dubiosity
Disillusioned
Distorted

Standalone Romantic Mystery:
The Good Girl

Suspense:
Imperfect
The Wrecking

Sweet Christmas Novella:
Home to Chestnut Grove

Standalone Romantic-Suspense:
Keeping Guard

The Last Target

Race Against Time

Ricochet

Key Witness

Lifeline

High-Stakes Holiday Reunion

Desperate Measures

Hidden Agenda

Mountain Hideaway

Dark Harbor

Shadow of Suspicion

The Baby Assignment

The Cradle Conspiracy

Trained to Defend

Mountain Survival

Nonfiction:

Characters in the Kitchen

Changed: True Stories of Finding God through Christian Music (out of print)

The Novel in Me: The Beginner's Guide to Writing and Publishing a Novel (out of print)

USA Today has called Christy Barritt's books "scary, funny, passionate, and quirky."

Christy writes both mystery and romantic suspense novels that are clean with underlying messages of faith. Her books have won the Daphne du Maurier Award for Excellence in Suspense and Mystery, have been twice nominated for the Romantic Times Reviewers' Choice Award, and have finaled for both a Carol Award and Foreword Magazine's Book of the Year.

She is married to her Prince Charming, a man who thinks she's hilarious—but only when she's not trying to be. Christy is a self-proclaimed klutz, an avid music lover who's known for spontaneously bursting into song, and a road trip aficionado.

When she's not working or spending time with her family, she enjoys singing, playing the guitar, and exploring small, unsuspecting towns where people have no idea how accident-prone she is.

Find Christy online at:
www.christybarritt.com
www.facebook.com/christybarritt
www.twitter.com/cbarritt

Sign up for Christy's newsletter to get information on all of her latest releases here: **www. christybarritt.com/newsletter-sign-up/**